T0156873

Crystal
Balls

Crystal Balls

"There is a fabric to the universe,
and sometimes you get caught on a loose thread."

Bill Rogers · Steve Mueller

iUniverse, Inc.
Bloomington

CRYSTAL BALLS

iUniverse books may be ordered through booksellers or by contacting:

iUniverse
1663 Liberty Drive
Bloomington, IN 47403
www.iuniverse.com
1-800-Authors (1-800-288-4677)

Because of the dynamic nature of the Internet, any web addresses or links contained in this book may have changed since publication and may no longer be valid. The views expressed in this work are solely those of the author and do not necessarily reflect the views of the publisher, and the publisher hereby disclaims any responsibility for them.

Any people depicted in stock imagery provided by Thinkstock are models, and such images are being used for illustrative purposes only.

Certain stock imagery © Thinkstock.

ISBN: 978-1-4759-7239-9 (hc)
ISBN: 978-1-4759-7238-2 (sc)
ISBN: 978-1-4759-7240-5 (e)

Library of Congress Control Number: 2013901010

Printed in the United States of America

iUniverse rev. date: 2/19/2013

for Shirley

Special thanks to Bobby Rotenberg for invaluable
guidance with the writing process, and of course
to my late collaborator Steve Mueller.

CONTENTS

CHAPTER 1

Getting Out There

The coffee mug on Roger's desk cast a shadow sideways, and it gave him an uneasy feeling in his gut. When he sat down this morning to write his column for the newspaper, the sun was coming through the front window, so the shadow pointed straight at him. Now, after a day of solitary work, punctuated only by expeditions to the kitchen or bathroom, the sun was shining in from the side balcony. That was how he marked time—the gradual shifting of sunlight and shadows. The rest of the world was out there leading normal lives, going to normal jobs, with people and clocks and subway whistles. And here he was, working alone and living alone. The feeling of isolation washed over him like a tidal wave of garbage water. He didn't want to end up like one of those psychos who went naked up the bell tower with an assault rifle and was described later on the six o'clock news as *"quiet, kept to himself."*

He took the mug into the kitchen. The dried mudflat of coffee at the bottom required an extra swash with the soapy sponge. The hot water felt good on his hands. He put the mug on the dish rack and went out to the balcony for some air. It was an ordinary April afternoon, or so it seemed.

From the tenth floor, he could see the horizon to the west. To the south, he saw the skyscrapers of downtown Toronto and the oceanic lake beyond. Below, on the sidewalk, he noticed something typical of this upscale yet hip neighborhood known as The Annex: a middle-aged mother in a psychedelic dress and Birkenstocks pushing an eight-hundred-dollar baby stroller. Her breasts probably produced foamed milk for baby lattes.

He couldn't afford any of that on the money he was making as a freelance writer. This concerned him. He was thirty, but compared to his friends, he wasn't doing much better than a twelve-year-old with a lawn-mowing business. His hopes were riding on the novel he was working on. It had been eight years since he started it. He didn't believe in rushing things.

He sighed and gazed toward the sun. It glinted off his blond hair. He was dressed in his usual outfit: a button-down shirt, jeans, and a tweed blazer. Checking his watch, he thanked God the time had finally come to go meet three of his buddies at The Labyrinth, a nearby coffee shop whose pointy Victorian roof was visible in the distance.

He took the elevator down and emerged onto the sidewalk, where he walked west into what would soon become a spectacular orange-and-red sunset. His anxiety about the isolation of the writer's life suddenly shifted to a niggling worry about crowds. Would he and his three buddies find a table at The Labyrinth? It was a popular place, especially on a Friday afternoon. It was one of a kind, not part of a big chain. You could get fancy and exotic coffees there.

He told himself to stop worrying. He focused on a pleasant thought—Sarah, the lovely red-haired waitress who was The Labyrinth's biggest attraction for him. He'd had a crush on her for months, but he remained reluctant to ask her out. The advice of his high school teacher still haunted him: "Wait until you're *somebody* before you think about getting married." His current career situation didn't make him feel very eligible.

If only life were as malleable as words, he thought. When he was writing, he could control events and people. He was captain of a ship in fair weather. But when he left the safety of his computer, he was in a storm at sea—a cabin boy on a garbage scow stuck in the Bermuda Triangle. Still, no matter how frustrating life could be, he was determined to fight for control against the currents and swells.

The route to The Labyrinth cut through a park. The leaves were starting to turn the trees green, and purple crocuses glowed in the afternoon light. The sweet scent of blossoms was in the air. As Roger followed the path, he noticed a noise coming from behind. It sounded like a squeaky wheel. He also heard a man talking, apparently to himself, in a gruff and peculiar voice.

Roger peered back over his shoulder and saw him—a weird hobo pushing a rusted shopping cart, which appeared to be his sole companion on this earth. It was filled with unidentifiable stuff. What looked like rotten lettuce leaves dangling from a hole in the bottom might have actually been the corner of a blanket that had seen better days. He wore a battered overcoat. It was filthy and torn, and at one particular area on its front, it looked as if someone had set a fire there and then put that fire out with Dijon mustard. His pants weren't pants at all, but old pajama bottoms. They were not clean, nor were they fully intact. His shoes were battered leather clodhoppers the size of rowboats. His face was carved into a semitoothless grin. His head was crowned with a makeshift aluminum-foil hat.

The words coming out of his mouth seemed like gibberish: "Brewed, brewed in a cat's butt," he sputtered. "The guy has a big meaning-of-life secret. Oh, the girl with the walnut eyes."

Roger tried not to listen, but the soliloquy cut through the air with strange clarity. "The fake clairvoyant is made real, and the suits take journeys. One will un-Jesus his church and have a Scottish demon foisted upon him. Another will eat magic. The spirit guide is the worm … or the madman? The fabric brings all threads together."

The hobo drew nearer. He seemed to be looking right at Roger. It was frightening. Roger quickened his pace. The hobo sped up too. Roger began to sweat. He turned toward the park gate, walking faster and faster until he emerged onto the sidewalk. He glanced back and breathed a sigh of relief—the hobo had stayed on the park path and soon vanished out of sight.

Roger wiped the sweat off his brow. His beloved coffee shop came into view—an old brick building that had once been a stately private home. A green oval wooden sign hung out over the sidewalk with "The Labyrinth" painted on it in white letters. It was one of the busiest corners of The Annex where, as was typical, a treed residential street ran headlong into a commercial thoroughfare. It was full of students, writers, and the lords and ladies of expensive real estate. Roger smiled.

CHAPTER 2

Enter the Labyrinth

At the entrance to The Labyrinth, several boys, about ten years old or so, were playing, laughing, and spraying cans of Silly String at each other. Silly String! Roger hadn't seen it in years. Mounds of the multicolored stuff had accumulated at the threshold. He stepped through it and into the coffee shop.

Surveying the room, he saw that it was just as he'd feared—the place was packed, all abustle with customers and servers. The din of many separate and animated conversations converged into a caffeine-charged fugue of human voices. It hit Roger like a tidal wave, and although it jarred him momentarily, it ultimately had a soothing effect. It was just the antidote for the cabin fever he had been enduring.

The air was pleasantly thick with the aroma of fresh-ground coffee and cinnamon buns. Vintage tungsten lightbulbs glowed a pale yellow in antique chandeliers, and old black-and-white photographs of historic Toronto adorned the walls. Above a stone fireplace hung a painting of a classical Greek labyrinth: a circular maze with a mythical Minotaur—half man, half bull—trapped at the center. The floors were hardwood, and the bar was solid walnut buffed to a glossy polish. Roger spotted the back of his best friend's head at the far side of the room.

It was Karl. There was no mistaking him. Karl's hair was jet-black and hung in tight bushy curls down past his shoulders. He wore a faded denim jacket with "Live to Ride" emblazoned across the back in red letters. His jeans fit snugly over well-worn leather boots. Wrapped tight around his head was a black bandanna dotted with white skulls and crossbones. It looked like a sky full of evil stars.

Roger navigated through the servers, who were weaving around like tightrope walkers balancing trays of coffee, pastries, and sandwiches. He approached Karl from behind. Karl, without turning around, spoke. "Hey, Little Buddy!"

"Hey, Skipper," replied Roger as he rounded the table and came into view. "How's it going?"

"All is well. And you?"

"Not bad," said Roger. "I just saw a really weird homeless guy in the park. Freaked me out. He was wearing an aluminum-foil hat."

"The dude with the shopping cart?"

"You've seen him?"

"Yeah. He stands on the street corner sometimes and makes weird hand gestures, like he's tugging at invisible strings."

"Crazy?"

"Seems like. Then again, what if there really *are* strings that we can't see, and he really *is* pulling on them and reeling stuff in?"

Roger laughed.

"I talked to him once," Karl continued. "He calls himself Spud."

"Spud. What's with his hat?"

"Aluminum foil, man. Protects his brain from thought-controlling radio waves from the government."

Roger sat down and noticed something strange on his shoe. "I've got Silly String on me. The kids playing by the door are spraying the stuff around." He shook it off. "Good thing it doesn't really stick, much."

"I had the same issue," said Karl. "Some of it got onto my boot. Funny how it doesn't stick. So I am entanglement-free."

"Shall we partake of the fine selection of coffees?" asked Roger with mock pomposity. "Perhaps a Guatemalan organic roast? An excellent beverage for the coffee connoisseur."

"Wait," said Karl with a mischievous smirk. He picked up a promotional coffee menu that had been sitting on the table, perched upright in a clear plastic display holder. "Check this out." He began reading: *"Luwak coffee—a rare and elegant brew. The digestive juices of the animal mellow the coffee."*

"Digestive juices?" said Roger, scowling. "Is that the stuff where the coffee beans have been eaten and crapped out by an African weasel?"

"No. It says here it gets crapped out by wild Indonesian cats. It's eight bucks a cup."

"For cat droppings? We could go to your grandma's house and dig through the litter box for free. Forget Luwak coffee. No way I'm gonna drink it."

"Definitely not."

A waitress approached. It was Sarah. She was poised and slightly aloof. Her red hair flowed gracefully down to her shoulders. Her hazel eyes seemed to sparkle like Egyptian jewels. When she smiled, which was often, she had the beauty of a model or an actress.

"Hi, guys," she said. "What can I get you? I know you like the Guatemalan organic, but we've got a special on Luwak today. I'm supposed to push it. Manager's orders."

"I'll have the Luwak," Roger said, without hesitation. He gestured to Karl. "And him too."

Sarah smiled. "I thought you might. I'll go see what I can squeeze out of Fluffy." As she turned and walked away, the guys watched her appreciatively.

"Man, she is so cool," said Roger.

"Yeah, she's so cool that we're going to get botulism from drinking the product of a cat's behind." Karl shook his head disdainfully, but he couldn't conceal his smirk. "She's a college student or something, isn't she?"

"Law. Law school. Totally out of my league. She's so pretty. The worst part is she's even smarter than she is pretty. And she's even sweeter than she is smart."

"And that's bad because?"

"In five years, she'll be earning more money in a month than I make all year. And she'll still be pretty, and she'll still be smart. Totally out of my league."

"In five years, that might be true," Karl replied. "But you never know where you'll be in a week, do you? Maybe she'll take you with her."

Roger shook his head and smiled at the thought. He would like nothing better than to be taken on a journey with Sarah. But it didn't fit into his grand plan: become somebody and *then* find somebody. He examined the Luwak card again. Cat-crap coffee! Why had he ordered it? Of course, he knew the answer. She was perfect. Worth drinking beverages from a cat's butt.

He noticed something else lying on the table. It wasn't a coffee menu; it was an advertising leaflet. It said, *"Psychic Demonstration Today—Come Experience the Astounding Anya Dreamchaser, God-gifted Medium and Clairvoyant!"* He laughed and showed it to Karl.

"Check this out, dude. Psychic demonstration. Maybe we should go and find out why we're drinking cat-crap coffee."

"I think we both know why we ordered Fluffy's bum-nectar," said Karl. "Or, should I say, why *you* ordered it."

Roger shrugged and smiled. "A psychic demonstration. I wonder what goes on at those things. I've always wanted to check that stuff out."

Karl examined the leaflet. "You really want to go to a psychic demonstration?" he asked coyly. "A real one?"

"Maybe it'll be a window on another world."

"Well, that's the thing about windows. You can look out of them, but you can fall out of them too. And you just never know where you'll land. Are you up for that kind of adventure, Little Buddy? You wanna take a peek into the crystal balls?"

"What do you mean crystal *balls*? Isn't it usually just one?"

"Just one ball? Now, that just doesn't work, on so many levels. Besides, more than one ball, more than one view."

Roger scratched his head. "What do *you* know about this stuff?"

Before Karl could answer, Gregory arrived at the table. "Good afternoon, Gentlemen," he said. He was prim, proper, and stuffy—a proverbial "suit," dressed in a good-quality blue pinstripe and red silk tie. He was a lawyer in a big downtown firm, handling big-money deals for cigar-smoking bigwigs. His posture was excellent. He could have walked a mile with a Bible balanced on his head. His face was friendly but serious, and his long neck and pointy nose made him vaguely resemble an ostrich.

"I can't believe those darned kids," he complained, trying unsuccessfully to shake Silly String off his heel. "That stuff is everywhere. My whole day has been like this. On days like today, I think I should have listened to my mother and gone into the priesthood."

"Priesthood?" said Roger, surprised.

"It's hard to imagine you in the pulpit!" Karl laughed.

"I was raised Catholic," Gregory retorted, seeming suddenly pious and defensive.

"I didn't know you were a spiritual man," said Roger.

"*Spiritual* is a big word," Gregory replied, with a whiff of smug condescension. "Let's just say that even though I don't go to church anymore, I have been following a higher path. I always knew I would do important work."

Karl's mouth dropped open. "*Important work?* You're a corporate lawyer, not Mother Teresa."

"Listen, what I do is important. There aren't many people who know how to take a company public."

"Okay, Pope Gregory," said Karl.

They all laughed.

Ralph arrived at the table to complete the foursome. He too had Silly String on his shoe. He was trying in vain to kick it loose. "Hey, boys," he said. "I'm tangled in those kids' stringy stuff. On a brighter note, I've just devised another brilliant tax shelter scheme, if I do say so myself."

He took off his Armani jacket and designer cuff links made of hematite, which caught Karl's attention. Ralph's curly brown hair hung down below his collar, and his round wire-rimmed eyeglasses softened his appearance. He wasn't a stuffed shirt like Gregory, although he had been a lawyer of the same ilk—before he jumped ship from his downtown firm to be a financial wizard.

"Sounds like fun," said Karl, "getting paid for dreaming up tax schemes. Roger and I should get jobs in finance."

"You two could never handle the corporate life," Ralph retorted. "Since when do either of you care about money and, more importantly, having lots of it, like any sane man? You guys don't live in the real world. You're too *out there*."

"We are not," Roger protested.

"He's right," said Karl. "We are 'out there.'"

"Why?"

"The view is better."

Sarah appeared with two Luwaks. "Here you go. The most expensive coffee ever made." Roger and Karl made a show of rubbing their hands in anticipation. She turned to Gregory and Ralph. "What can I get you?"

Ralph looked at the Luwaks. "What's this stuff?"

"The finest coffee available to humanity," Roger interjected. "On special for eight bucks a cup. Made from coffee beans that have been crapped out by wild Indonesian cats." He pointed to the menu card. "Check it out."

"That's disgusting," said Ralph.

"Don't be narrow-minded," said Roger. "This is a new taste sensation." He raised the mug to his nose and took a whiff and then a sip. "Mmm. Tastes like the forest." Everyone laughed, including Sarah. "Actually," said Roger, "it's good. Mellow. The smoothest coffee I've ever tasted."

Karl tried his. "Yeah," he said. "It goes down nicely. I do like a smooth coffee."

"You want to try it?" asked Sarah, looking at Gregory and Ralph. "I'm on a mission to sell the stuff. Manager's orders."

"I dare ya," said Roger.

Karl whispered aside to Sarah: "Bring another pair of Luwaks for these gentlemen." She was gone before they could protest.

"Okay," said Ralph, annoyed. "I guess we're drinking cat-crap coffee today." He scooped his cuff links off the table and noticed the psychic's leaflet. "What's this?"

"Psychic demonstration," said Roger.

"What a load of crap," said Ralph. "Just like our coffee."

Roger peered over at the leaflet. "It's happening in forty-five minutes. Right down the street. At the university. Wanna go? Who's in?"

"Great idea," said Ralph sarcastically. "I'll drink cat crap, then I'll go see more crap."

Gregory grabbed the leaflet and examined it. "Pathetic. I feel sorry for anyone who would believe this stuff. It's the opiate of the stupid, nothing more."

"Come on, guys," said Roger. "Let's go. It's free, it's nearby, and it'll be good for a laugh. I need material for my next column."

"I wouldn't go if you paid me," said Ralph.

"Me neither," said Gregory.

Karl said nothing.

"I've got an idea," said Roger. "Let's make a bet. We'll go check it out. If this Anya Dreamchaser is a fake, I will buy your coffees for the next month. Including Luwak, if you so desire. But if she's real, you'll buy my coffees for the next month. Including Luwak. Which I very well might be ordering because I like this stuff." He nodded and took a sip.

"You are ridiculous," said Gregory.

"Wait a second," said Ralph. "This sounds like a good bet." He poked his index finger into Roger's chest. "Count me in. There's a sucker born every minute."

"Well, all right," agreed Gregory. "I suppose it might be amusing. I'm in."

Karl remained quiet, looking away. He seemed uncomfortable. Sarah appeared with two Luwaks and set them down. Gregory and Ralph made faces and then took reluctant sips.

"Not bad, actually," said Ralph.

The guys bantered for a while longer, finished their coffees, put down their money, and left for the show. As they walked toward the door, they didn't notice Sarah and another coffee shop staffer, Wanda, watching them.

"My, my, my," said Wanda. "Ya know, ya just couldn't say which one is cutest." She sighed approvingly. "None of their girlfriends are with them today."

"They don't all have girlfriends," Sarah replied.

"How do you know?"

"They've been coming here for a while. The two suits have girlfriends for sure. I've seen them." Then she gestured toward Roger. "But the cute one doesn't, at least not that I've ever seen." She pointed at Karl. "Neither does the spooky one."

"With four great butts like that, how am I supposed to know which one's the cute one?"

"You know, the *cute* one? The nice one? Hello? The cute, smart one?"

"Looks like somebody has a crush!"

Sarah blushed. "He writes the *City Life* column for the paper. His name's Roger. He's really funny."

"A writer, eh? How romantic."

As Sarah finished clearing the table, she looked up at the television behind the coffee bar. There was a science documentary on. She watched for a moment. A military man was being interviewed.

"Thanks for being on the program, Captain Buford Mayhew.

We've heard the US military has used psychics in the past, and they may still be using them. You had direct experience with this during the Cold War. Tell us about it."

"Ah believe they were for real," said Captain Mayhew in a thick Texas accent. He had a friendly face, a gray brush cut, and a sturdy square jaw. "I saw it with my own eyes. If you don't believe, then tell me: how could those men, in a basement in Colorado, draw the details of a Siberian missile silo in the Kamchatka Peninsula, before we saw the telemetry? I want to know!"

Sarah shrugged and gave the table a final wipe.

CHAPTER 3

The Showstopper

The psychic demonstration was being held in one of the university's old buildings, a majestic nineteenth-century stone structure that looked more like a mansion than a school. It was topped with a cone-shaped spire of red clay tile, surrounded by four smaller stone turrets, each wrapped with bands of darker red rock. The walls were covered with ivy. Windows of leaded glass peered out through the foliage like friendly eyes.

Above the door there was a grand archway with "THE TRUTH SHALL MAKE YOU FREE" carved into the stone in block letters. Back when Roger had been a student here, studying philosophy, the last "E" in "FREE" was partially obscured by ivy. He thought it was a "T."

The courtyard out front had an ornamental reflecting pool. A little boy was sitting on the edge. He had been playing with some toy plastic dogs, which were spread out in front of him. Now he was busy weaving a cat's cradle. The light from the setting sun made the water sparkle. The boy stood up, pleased with himself, and accidentally knocked one of his toy dogs—a Saint Bernard—into the water.

Roger and the guys walked past the pool toward the entrance. Gregory was skeptical. "I can't believe we're doing this," he said.

"A month of free Luwaks," chimed Ralph.

Karl said nothing.

The guys entered and saw there was a good turnout—students, civilians, and a few eccentric types. One guy was wearing incredibly dark glasses and had a long, white ponytail. He looked like a mad professor.

The first thing Roger did was go to a makeshift snack counter that had been set up for the event. He was surprised to see they were selling little bags of Diamond-brand walnuts, which came with disposable plastic nutcrackers. *How odd,* he thought. *Who buys walnuts during a show?* He decided to do so. He rejoined the group, and they walked together down the hall to the auditorium.

Karl took an aisle seat. Roger sat beside him, looking relaxed, taking in the ambience of the room with his bag of walnuts on his lap. Ralph and Gregory sat in the next two seats and began to chuckle smugly.

Karl seemed nervous. "I hate these things," he muttered quietly. "They always turn me on."

"Turn you on?" Roger said.

Karl realized he had spoken aloud and been heard. "Er, well, crystal balls and all."

The lights dimmed, and the emcee appeared on stage. His silver hair had been gussied up into a pompadour. His suit was gray, and he wore round eyeglasses with thick, dark plastic frames. He looked like a game show host.

"Ladies and Gentlemen," he said, "welcome to part three of our ongoing series on the paranormal. I'm thrilled to be here this evening to introduce author, teacher, psychic extraordinaire: Anya Dreamchaser!"

To polite applause, Anya took the stage. She was not unattractive, although she did seem rather flamboyant in her layers of scarves and loose-fitting peasant shawls. She wore an abundance of silver jewelry and a large crystal pin on her forehead to secure her turban. She also wore a pendant of a cat and Birkenstocks with wool socks. She was affecting an aura of serenity.

"Welcome, seekers of truth. I am about to share with you the secrets of the past, present, and future. You may find the experience overwhelming. If you need help digesting it all, there are copies of my book, *The Meaning of Life: One Woman's Journey*, available at the door." She held up a copy. It looked amateurish, probably self-published, with a years-out-of-date, highly retouched black-and-white photo of her on the cover.

"And if you like games of chance, I have a selection of lucky gambling talismans." She held up a cheap gold-colored chain with slot-machine and four-leafed-clover charms on it. "These are assembled for me personally by the Celestial Cooperative Collective."

Ralph and Gregory were trying not to snort with derision, while Roger rummaged around his bag of walnuts. Karl fidgeted uncomfortably.

"And now," Anya continued, "I am sad to say that I am a widow woman. But no need to feel sorrow for me. My beloved life partner, Thomas, is with me still. Our love crosses the barrier between life and death. He helps me see into the souls of my clients—er, seekers."

She asked for a volunteer from the audience. A young Chinese woman stood up and went onto the stage. Anya gestured welcomingly to her, breathed deeply, and took hold of both her hands, all the while keeping her eyes on the audience.

"Clients!" said Ralph. "She actually said clients! This is crap." He looked smugly over at Roger.

Anya held the volunteer's hands. "I'm seeing something," she said.

Ralph and Gregory were trying to contain their laughter. Roger was attempting to crack a walnut without making noise. Karl peered toward the stage, shaking his head no.

"Is it my dead mother who I am missing so much?" the volunteer asked.

"Not so fast," said Anya. "I'm seeing a female parent figure."

"My mother?"

"Yes!" Anya turned to the audience. "I know my book would help you with this problem. Oh, my dear, I am so glad I'm going to be able to help you learn to forgive your mother. With my humble book. Which can be purchased at the door."

Anya asked the volunteer for a personal article and was given a gold chain. Karl fidgeted and knocked a walnut out of Roger's hands. Roger elbowed him.

"What's your problem?" Roger whispered, searching the floor for his walnut.

Karl appeared to be listening to someone else. "Okay, okay, I get it," he muttered, apparently to thin air.

This drew Anya's attention. "Ahem. Excuse me, Gentlemen?" she said, smiling and making a "turn-it-down" gesture. "You're disrupting the celestial harmonies. I don't expect you to understand, but you must trust me. I need silence to be able to help this poor, poor girl."

The emcee stood up and added peevishly, "Son, this isn't some frat party or rave or some hippie-dippie 'happening.' People come here for genuine psychic guidance. You are distracting us."

Karl's eyes kept darting to an empty place on the stage. Unable to stop himself, he began speaking out loud, "Okay, I get it."

Anya became even more annoyed. "Ladies and Gentlemen, this man obviously feels left out. Don't be angry with him." She aimed her gaze directly at Karl. "Son, we can't all be God-gifted, which I am blessed to be. But I forgive you. I understand. If you'd like to learn how to release your own psychic abilities, you can find further guidance in my book."

The emcee piped up. "I think even a negative and closed-minded person might benefit from Madam Anya's teachings. She brings us true psychic gifts, not some crystal-ball chicaneries."

Anya looked Karl in the eye: "The only crystal balls in the room tonight, young man, you must have brought in yourself."

Karl turned to Roger. "Man, I wish I didn't have to do this." He stood up. "Ma'am, I don't mean to be rude, but she doesn't need to forgive her mother. She wants to know if her mom forgave *her*, for not coming home when she got sick. And you're just ... you're just, well, trying to sell her one of your stupid books."

Karl suddenly seemed more imposing than usual. His resemblance to a member of the Hell's Angels only added to the general sense of foreboding. With his long hair flowing from under his skull bandanna, he strode up onto the stage. He peered at the volunteer. Then he glanced back at an empty space, as though watching someone no one else could see. He gently took the gold chain from Anya's hand. He quivered briefly but noticeably. He looked down at the volunteer, who was clearly displeased by this turn of events. He squinted at her while squeezing the gold chain.

"There's someone here who wants to talk to you in the worst way," he said. "It's your mom." Karl began rolling words around in his mouth. "Pretty ... green ... stone ... on ... winter's ... blanket?"

The volunteer's jaw dropped. "Oh my god. Oh my god!"

"Jade?" he said. "Jade! Jade and snow?"

"Yes! That's my name in Mandarin! Jade Snow! My mother call me that at home! Yes, yes, my mother call me that! Oh to be sure, thank you kindly."

Karl peered at her more intensely. Then, to someone unseen, he said, "Yes, um ... yes, yes, I hear you." He turned to Jade. "And, your mother, something was wrong with her." He lifted his left hand. "Her left hand. I can't feel her left hand."

"Yes! Mother lose hand in dollar-store toy factory. No extra pay, nothing. Had to take crummy one-handed jobs after."

"Jade Snow," said Karl, speaking slowly, "you were very brave when you fought the other children who called your mother 'Old Missus One-Hand Jobs.'"

Jade nodded in wonder.

"Mother says you needed to get your education," he continued. "That's all she ever wanted for you. She was not hurt that you didn't go back home when she got sick. Your two, no, three brothers looked after her very well. She wanted school for you. And she loves you very much."

Jade started sobbing. "Yes, all it's true! All it's true. Three brothers, one-hand mother, me, and school! And, she not mad? She not mad!"

The audience was riveted. Gregory and Ralph were staring, perplexed. Roger was awed but loving it. He cracked open a walnut, the only sound in the room.

Jade frowned and pointed at Anya. "That woman dressed like laundry, nothing she said meant anything, not anything. Oh, poor my Missus One-Hand Job. Mommy, Mommy."

Karl turned to Anya. "There's someone here for you too." She stood nervously still. "It's Tim ... No, Tom. Wow. You *did* have a husband named Thomas ... No, he says. 'Tom.' Very particular on that point. Oh, he's pissed at you, Anya. Really pissed ... What? ... Oh. He says, not that he *could* piss, at the end."

Anya gasped.

"He says his prostate doesn't hurt anymore." Karl listened a bit more and then giggled. "But you're still a pain in the ass."

Anya turned white.

"And he says you've been hurting people with these fake psychic readings, Anya, when you could be doing the real thing." Karl squinted. "He wants me to flick on your psychic switch. Hey, you really do have quite a switch, there. Yeah, I guess I could do it. Never did it before, but Tom here is showing me."

Karl concentrated. Anya's eyes slowly widened in confusion. In the black depths of her pupils, there was a sudden, almost imperceptible motion. She turned to the empty place on the stage. "T-T-T-Tom!" she cried. "No, this can't be!"

The audience watched in awe as Anya began waving madly about, as though fending off someone who was trying to embrace her. She hurried off the stage and fled, knocking a pile of her books and lucky talismans to the floor. After she exited the auditorium, her voice could still be heard in the distance: "No, no, this can't be happening."

The emcee got up and walked toward Karl with his finger pointed in accusation. Karl, blinking and looking dazed, stepped toward him with one hand gently outstretched. "It's okay," Karl said softly. "It's nothing to be ashamed of. My grandfather wore them too. They're not noticeable. It's a medical condition."

The emcee's eyes widened in horror as he dropped his hands below his waist and felt his backside. He scrambled to collect his notes, briefcase, and overcoat and then leaped off the stage and ran for the door. As he departed, he announced as fast as he could speak: "Ladies and Gentlemen, that's all for tonight." He stumbled over the spilled heap of Anya's books. "Help yourself to a free copy of *The Meaning of Life: One Woman's Journey.*"

The houselights came on. The audience began murmuring excitedly to one another. Then they began leaving, stepping over Anya's books on the floor. No one picked up a copy.

Karl shook his head and stared out at the auditorium, which was now empty except for the guys. "Man," he said. "I hate when this happens."

Gregory and Ralph were slack-jawed. Roger had a look of happy wonder on his face. "What the heck is in that cat crap?" he said. There was a crack as he opened another walnut.

CHAPTER 4

Deep Thoughts

Outside the auditorium, the sun was nearly gone, and the western sky glowed red. The guys emerged from the building and mustered by the pool.

"Holy crap!" said Ralph, looking agitated. "What just happened?"

"Yeah," said Gregory, with a pained and solemn expression on his face.

They both stared at Karl.

"That was awesome!" Roger cried, with a juvenile smile. "Talking to dead people!"

"Easy, Little Buddy," Karl retorted. "Let's head back to The Labyrinth. We can talk there."

Suddenly a ringtone sounded, and Ralph pulled out his phone. "I gotta take this call. You guys go ahead."

"I'll wait here too," said Gregory, pulling out his own phone. "We'll see you there."

"All right," said Karl. He strode off. Roger followed with a spring in his step.

"Man, that was so cool!" said Roger. "You really are 'out there.' How could you not tell me you were psychic?"

"You didn't ask."

"I've never seen anyone do anything like that before."

"I keep it to myself, dude. I used to let people see it. I used to do psychic readings at parties. Years ago. I would tell people about their past and their future. But they would make fun of me. Or get hostile. Especially if I didn't tell them what they wanted to hear. That's why I don't do it anymore."

"This changes everything, dude!" cried Roger. "I mean, I've never been spiritual, but I always wanted to be. I kinda had my own religion, you know?"

"Religion? You mean when you'd get drunk and ask me about how the universe started? Or do you mean how you watched *The X-Files* religiously?"

"Very funny. Seriously, I feel like I missed out. My dad came from a long line of Protestant atheists, and my mom was a churchgoer when she was a kid, but I never saw her set foot in one. I should start going. Maybe they'll come out with a religion that celebrates the Sabbath on Wednesday so it won't wreck my weekends."

"I admire your spiritual commitment."

Roger glanced back at Gregory and Ralph. In the distance, he could see they were still at the pool, on their phones. "They seem a bit freaked out," Roger said.

"It happens. A cup of Luwak should straighten them out. Distract them, anyway."

"How long have you been psychic?"

"Ever since I can remember. It's really just a sixth sense. I wish there was a guidebook to go with it. But there's not."

"Maybe you should write the guidebook. Maybe it would be better if guys like you who actually have the ability wrote the books and not frauds like Anya."

"There are some honest books out there," Karl replied. "I've seen a few. But psychic talents are too unreliable, too unpredictable. It's like guessing which thread to pull at the carnival sideshow game. Pull the right thread, and you get the giant panda for your girlfriend. But you're far more likely to pull one of the three hundred other threads." Out of his pocket, he pulled one of Anya's abandoned good-luck charms. "And then you just win a piece of tin jewelry crap."

"Wrong thread?"

Karl nodded.

"What do you do when you finally find the right thread?"

"Recognize it for what it is. Jump on it. Ride it. Ride the thread until you get wherever it's supposed to lead you."

"What if it isn't taking you anywhere important?"

"It rarely is, Little Buddy; it rarely is. But you just ride it anyway. Otherwise, you get tangled up. Like picking away at a loose thread in a favorite sweater. Gets it all unraveled and tangled. Better to just go along with it."

They arrived back at The Labyrinth. Sarah noticed them come in. She seemed surprised. As she approached, Roger intercepted her and ordered four Luwaks. She beamed.

They sat down. "So, dude," said Karl. "The weekend is finally upon us. You still up for our road trip north? I talked to my grandma, and it's all good. We can stay at her place. Right near Casino Rama."

"For sure!" said Roger. "It'll be fun. I love casinos."

Karl pulled one of Anya Dreamchaser's talismans, a metal four-leaf clover, from his pocket. "You feel lucky, mister?"

"Not from that piece of crap!" Roger laughed. Then his eyes suddenly widened as an idea occurred to him. "Dude, have you ever tried to 'ride the thread' through a casino? Or lotteries? Or horse races or something? Like, can we play with this?"

"That's right, Little Buddy," Karl retorted sarcastically. "I offer you proof that there are real psychics and that human spirits really do exist and that I can talk to the dead, and your response is: 'Cool, can we make a few bucks off of it?'"

Karl paused for a moment. "I tried horses. It didn't work. Can't pick lottery numbers, too confusing to look at numbers and get them right when you're looking into the future. Tried card games, but they're so fast-paced and distracting."

Roger wasn't discouraged. "Well, maybe you could just walk

up and down a room full of slot machines and pick out the ones that are about to pay off big."

Karl looked surprised at this notion.

"Look," Roger continued, "we could go to the casino, get a pail of coins, you could get all 'I-see-dead-peopled-up,' then we hit the slot-machine barn and harvest the treasure like two hungry chipmunks on a walnut farm."

Karl laughed.

Sarah appeared at the table with the Luwaks. She set them down with a smile and walked off. Karl grabbed his and took a sip. "My grandma's psychic too, dude. I have to warn you."

"Really?"

"Yup. It tends to run in families."

"Cool. Does she, like, do readings and stuff?"

"Nah. She'd think it undignified."

"I don't suppose she ever goes to the casino and uses her psychic powers to win big?"

"You have amazing powers of deduction, Little Buddy."

Roger looked at the floor.

"Grandma *does* go to the casino quite regularly but not to gamble," Karl explained. "They have art shows, craft and needlework fairs, stuff like that. She's a big sewing fiend. She enters sewing competitions. And she has become very fond of the performers who come to play there. Musicians mostly. She even turned her garage into a studio apartment. Rents it out to the touring acts." Karl sipped more coffee and smiled. "Thank you, Fluffy!"

"Hey, dude," Roger whispered, leaning closer. "Can you, like, ride the thread on our waitress?"

"*Read.* It's called 'reading.' Hmm. Now, which waitress? You mean the one who's out of your league?"

"You *are* psychic!"

Karl squinted across the room at Sarah. "Yeah, I'm still sort of opened-up from what happened at the show. Hmm."

Karl got a glazed look. Roger tried to suppress giggles. After a moment, Karl spoke. "I'm seeing eyeglasses. They're broken. No, chewed. Like, a dog chewed and chewed on the plastic parts. Tortoiseshell or mahogany-colored frames. Plastic. Walnut. Walnut-colored, for sure. Gwaggles? Oh. She calls them 'the walnut goggles.' Stylish. Expensive reading glasses that she really liked. And I think it's pretty recent. Like, maybe this year? Or maybe this month?"

Sarah approached the table. "Can I settle up with you guys? I'm almost done with my shift."

"Sure," said Roger, winking at Karl and then looking up at Sarah. Karl quickly reached over and tried to stop him, but it was too late. "I hope tips were good today," Roger blurted, "so you can get some new walnut goggles."

Sarah's jaw dropped. "How did *you* know? As a matter of fact, my dog Cassiopeia chewed them up." She noticed the blank look on Roger's face. "Cassiopeia. Like, the constellation? Like, astronomy? Hello? But how could you know? No one knows about the walnut goggles."

Roger didn't know what to say. After a moment's awkwardness, she gave them their bill and hurried off.

"See?" said Karl, perturbed. "Oh, you couldn't have listened to my warning, could you, Little Buddy? You gotta be careful of who you talk to about the *threads*, man. People who haven't seen it for themselves can get really upset about it. You got off lightly, with her." Karl sipped his coffee and sighed. "There's a reason every Gilligan has a Skipper. Consider that to be your hat-beating."

"Man, I might have overreached myself there, eh?"

"D'ya think?"

Ralph and Gregory arrived at the table.

"Hello, my friends," said Roger. "I took the liberty of ordering you guys some Luwak." He raised his own cup. "And I guess mine should go on your tab. So should Karl's, after what he did."

Ralph and Gregory sat down and huddled over their coffee.

"Fine, fine, you won the bet," said Gregory. He took a sip. "But I've got more important things on my mind at the moment."

He looked at Karl. "What happened back there? This is crazy. I've never seen anything like what you did."

"Yeah," chimed Ralph. "This is crazy."

"Crazy!" agreed Roger.

"Shake it off, boys; shake it off," said Karl. "Get a grip. Enjoy the view. Enjoy the Luwak."

Gregory put his mug down. "I don't know what Leanne is going to say when I tell her about this," he said, referring to his longtime girlfriend. "She's going to freak."

"Yeah," said Ralph, "I really need to talk to Wendy. She is a total nonbeliever, but this will really open her eyes!"

"Boys," said Karl, "do yourselves a favor, and just sit on it. Don't mention this to your girlfriends. If you talk, the best that happens is they laugh at you and decide I'm a bad influence. The worst that happens is they laugh at me and decide *you* are the bad influence."

Gregory and Ralph looked puzzled.

"I've warned you," said Karl. "Don't try to understand it. Accept that now you know something you didn't. Do that, and you'll be fine. But start obsessing about 'fate' and 'spirits' and the need to know the unknowable, and you'll end up getting your own little thread of destiny tangled into a knot. The free choice is yours to make." He sipped his coffee. "But I'd shut up."

"Karl's right," said Roger. "He's been through this before. We should listen to Karl, for sure. This is his turf."

Gregory and Ralph didn't seem convinced. They both announced that they had to go home. They threw money down and left.

Roger turned to Karl. "Are they going to be okay?"

"Time, I guess, will tell," Karl replied. "But I'd say the game is afoot."

CHAPTER 5

Trajectories

Roger took the long way home from The Labyrinth, sticking to the streets and avoiding the park. He didn't want to run into any more crazies, especially now that it was dark. The moon had risen in the eastern sky, and a few stars were visible.

The sidewalk was alive with people taking advantage of the clear and warm night, a welcome thing after a Toronto winter. If it weren't for having to get up early the next day for the road trip north, Roger and Karl would likely have stuck together and moved from the coffee shop to one of the adjacent taverns or perhaps gone to hear some live blues at a nearby bistro. Instead, they parted ways until morning.

As he wandered back toward his apartment building, the feeling of loneliness returned. How did he end up thirty and single? If he'd taken a sensible degree at university, like accounting, he wouldn't be in this mess. He would be *somebody*—somebody with a career, somebody who could have a girlfriend or even a wife and kids.

But no. He had insisted on trying to be a writer, an *artist*. And his plan wasn't working on schedule. He was supposed to have at least one best seller by now. He didn't even have a finished manuscript. He thought of Sarah. He smiled a bittersweet smile.

He tried to snap himself out of his despair by recalling the day's events. What had seemed like an ordinary April afternoon had certainly turned out *not* to be—the foil-hatted hobo, the cat-crap coffee, his best friend talking to the dead. This last item made him smile. The holy books he'd heard about, but of course had never read, weren't crap after all! He'd always found it hard to make sense of a universe with God and spirits in it, but it never seemed any easier with those things gone. Now, having seen proof that spirits existed, he felt excited.

The most exciting aspect was figuring out how to harness this for profit. He continued strolling, trying to formulate a plan. He looked down at the sidewalk and noticed the cracks in the cement and the multitude of tar-like circles of old gum, forming a disgusting black constellation. When he lifted his gaze, he found himself in front of Book City. A flash of an idea came to him. He went in to look for how-to gambling manuals. With his psychic friend's help, he planned to "win big" at the casino.

The place was busy with shoppers and browsers, and he threaded himself through and around the tables stacked with best sellers and new releases. He'd been there many times. He knew that books about gambling would be on the second floor, so he climbed the creaking old staircase.

Was he being shallow and frivolous? He pondered this question guiltily as he emerged at the top of the stairs. Shouldn't he be taking more seriously the fact that Karl had talked to the dead? Maybe. He would discuss the situation in depth with him during the car ride tomorrow. In the meantime, why not try to take advantage of the situation for personal gain?

He bought two books: *How to Beat the Casinos* and *Lotteries, Luck, and You.* He took them back to his apartment and perused them while watching TV. He couldn't make much sense of what he was reading, and he grew tired. He put the books down and prepared for bed.

Meanwhile, back at The Labyrinth, Sarah was clearing the last table and preparing to close up. Wanda came to help. Sarah told her about the walnut goggles incident. "They never seemed weird before," said Wanda. "I always liked the 'Great Butt Four.' That's what I call 'em. Four really great butts, all at one table. Did you tell anyone else about your broken glasses? Anyone who might have told them?"

"No," replied Sarah. "But Roger knew about them somehow."

"Listen," said Wanda. "The one thing I *do* know about those guys is they seem like straight shooters. Whatever it is, I'm sure it will make sense once you've heard the whole story."

"I hope so. I'm definitely going to ask Roger about it."

"In the meantime, how about our weekend romp? When do you want to leave?"

"How about nine thirty? I've got my gym bag already packed."

"Perfect. I am so pumped! I love Casino Rama. This time, I'm going to hit the jackpot."

"Yeah," Sarah said, nodding. "What I love even more is the local First Nations artwork."

"Well, we'll win big, and we'll buy a ton of it."

"Check. Weekend: win big. Next week: talk to Roger."

Sarah turned out the lights, and they locked up The Labyrinth for the night.

Earlier, when Gregory left The Labyrinth, he went straight home to talk to Leanne. When he walked into their apartment, he saw her standing on her head.

"Hi, sweetie," he said.

"Hi," she replied, folding her slender body down and getting back on her feet. "I had a great yoga class today." She went to the fridge for a bottle of water, her bleach-blonde ponytail bouncing. When she returned to give Gregory a hello kiss, she noticed he seemed distracted.

"What's wrong, honey?"

"Nothing," he replied feebly.

"Really?"

"Well, Karl did something freaky."

"What happened?"

Gregory recounted the story.

"Wow," said Leanne. "Karl's an odd duck."

Gregory mused about religious topics throughout dinner: What was the nature of the afterlife? Why was there evil, if God was benevolent and all-powerful? During his childhood, he had been a devout Catholic. In his adulthood, that part of him withered until he eventually became entirely irreligious. Seeing Karl talk to the dead was a spark that reignited his inner spiritual fire.

Instead of joining Leanne after supper for some TV, Gregory retreated to the study and began searching for his Bible. Finally, he located the book—a scuffed, leather-bound volume given to him on the occasion of his confirmation as a Catholic. It was on the very top shelf, with all the other books that he seldom reached for. He needed a step stool to retrieve it. He dusted it off and cracked it open. The first thing he saw was a passage from Corinthians: "For God is not the author of confusion, but of peace." He sat in his leather desk chair and began to read. He became deeply immersed, drinking in the words like a desert weasel drinks water at an oasis.

Feelings of guilt began to grow inside him. Hours went by. Leanne finally turned off the TV and headed for bed. On the way there, she peeked in to the study and saw that Gregory had lit votive candles and dug out a portrait of a saint from the closet, which he had positioned in front of him. He was kneeling in prayer. She smiled and whispered, "Good night."

Meanwhile, Ralph was embarking on his own bizarre journey. When he got home, he told Wendy about what he had witnessed. "Spirits are real!" he cried. "Karl talked to them. I saw it. And if he can do it, *I* can do it!" He got a mischievous gleam in his eye. "I'm going to become a holy man!"

Wendy howled with laughter. "Oh great. Now I'm living with the Dalai Lama." She put her hands on her waist and glared dismissively. She was blessed with the beauty of a runway model— her jet-black hair cut in a bob, framing her perfect face. She was intimidating yet somehow approachable too.

Her disbelief represented a challenge to Ralph, who decided to demonstrate the wonders of the spirit world directly. "I'll prove it to you!" he cried. He darted off to the bedroom closet and dug out the Ouija board he'd had since he was a kid. The thing was marked with the letters of the alphabet, the numbers zero through nine, and the words *yes, no,* and *good-bye.* There was also a plastic heart-shaped tablet for the spirits to guide and spell out messages from the great beyond. He could remember trying it when he was little. It had been a tedious and pointless exercise back then. But now that he knew spirits were real, it would be different. He felt something amazing would happen.

"The Ouija board!" Wendy declared contemptuously.

"I know you're a skeptic, but you should give this a chance. I'm going to show you spirits exist. I am going to communicate with dead people."

"You've gone mad."

"Wendy, I'm telling you, I saw it with my own eyes. Karl talked to the dead."

"Okay," she laughed. "I'll watch your dog-and-pony show. Let me get some Milk Bones."

She sat down cross-legged on the rug opposite Ralph, who lit some candles. He put his fingers on the plastic tablet. He waited for the spirits to guide him. His fingers were trembling.

"I feel something moving," he said excitedly.

"Don't soil yourself," said Wendy.

Ralph seemed to feel his hands being pulled. Whether it was his imagination or a real occult force at work, he couldn't say.

After five excruciating minutes, the tablet pointed to the letter "L."

"L!" cried Ralph. "Cool! What do you think the next letter will be? What are the spirits trying to tell us?"

"I think I know," said Wendy.

"Really? What?"

"O."

"O," repeated Ralph pensively. "L and O. Maybe it will be the name *Lowell*. My dead uncle Lowell! He's trying to communicate with us."

"I think it's going to be a different word."

"What word?"

"Loser."

Ralph let out a laugh. "You have no faith."

Wendy stuck out her tongue at him. "Baby," she said, "I am exhausted. I need to go to bed. Tell Grandma I'll see her in heaven eventually, but I'll be arriving as late as possible." She kissed him good night.

Ralph smiled and sat back down at his Ouija board. He soon realized that if his hands moved, it was because *he* was moving them, not some supernatural force. He grew frustrated. It was the middle of the night, but he was wide awake. He walked over to the window. The sky was black, and he looked out at the twinkling lights of the city.

Meanwhile, Anya Dreamchaser was facing tribulations too. Having been "switched on" by Karl, she felt her life had suddenly become a cautionary tale. She was discovering how intrusive psychic visions could be. She wished she could turn it off, like a tap.

She decided to go to her regular hangout, a place called Tarot, Teas, 'n' Tarts. On her way there, Tom's ghost appeared again. He looked real, yet transparent. He floated alongside her as she walked.

"Honey," he said, "we need to talk."

"I can't believe you're here, Tom. It's freaking me out. I miss you so much. What's it like to be dead?"

"It's good."

"Good?"

"Yeah. Now honey, don't worry. You're going to be fine. That weird guy did something, and suddenly, I could communicate with you."

"No kidding. Tom, it's unbelievable."

"Anya, you don't have to fake it anymore."

"I don't think I want to keep doing psychic shows now that it's real. It's too weird."

"It was always real for you, honey, in a way. You could read people's feelings. Remember when we first met?"

"Of course."

"At the campus coffee shop at University of Toronto, remember? You were majoring in psychology, and I was just starting actuarial science. We were at the cream-and-sugar station. We both reached for the jug of half-and-half at the same time. Our hands touched. The jug was empty, and we laughed. I suggested mixing nonfat milk and full cream together, and you said you were going to do the same thing."

Anya smiled. "I remember."

"I was going through a hard time. You could tell. I wasn't sure being an actuary was a good road for me to go down."

"Yes," said Anya.

"Being an actuary turned out to be good for me. Just like you said it would."

"I could feel it, somehow," said Anya. "And I became a corporate psychologist. That was hard. Watching people pass the executive aptitude tests with flying colors, yet feeling in my heart they were on the wrong path."

"And you started wearing those shapeless canvas outfits, corduroy body stockings, and crazy loud muumuus."

"I thought you liked those."

"I liked some of them. They should never have fired you."

"It didn't matter in the end," said Anya, a tear welling in her eye. "Because when you passed away, the insurance money took care of me."

"Then you started doing your phony psychic readings."

"Yeah. I could tell what people were feeling. But the audience wanted more. So I started faking it."

"You don't have to fake it anymore, babe."

Tom's spirit drifted away.

"Tom! Come back!"

She started to cry.

She arrived at Tarot, Teas, 'n' Tarts and gazed at the window display of exotica and New Age books. She dried her eyes, opened the door, and entered. There was a coffee-and-cake counter along with several sofas. She nervously ordered a coffee and then turned to the sofas where several of her phony psychic colleagues were sitting.

There was a nervous-looking astrologer in jeans with a sparkly scarf wrapped around her head, sitting with a star chart on her lap. There was a pudgy youngish guy with a tarot card deck spread out on the coffee table. There were two middle-aged women stringing beads, both dressed in layers of loose-fitting shirts and scarves. They were taking children's art kits out of shopping bags from a local craft store, removing the plastic beads, and then stringing them onto elastic bands to make bracelets. Everyone nodded hello as Anya sat down.

"Oh, Anya, honey, where have you been?" said the astrologer. "You look like you've seen a ghost!" There was laughter all around.

"You're not going to believe this," Anya said. "I have seen a ghost. I've been talking to Tom … Yes, Tom!"

No one looked up from what they were doing.

"For real," Anya continued. "I really did see Tom. His spirit. I mean, for real."

The tarot-card guy spoke. "And how is that going over with the customers? Still working for ya?"

"No. No. This time, it was *real*."

"Of course it was," said the astrologer sarcastically. "What do you think of the new coffee they have here? It's exotic stuff. Really expensive. From Indonesia."

One of the bead stringers piped up. "I tried it. Tastes odd. Not like most coffee. Good, though."

"Really?" said the other bead stringer with disgust. "I thought it tasted like crap. I liked that walnut stuff they had last week."

Anya suddenly shifted her gaze to an empty space near the coffee counter. "He's back."

"Okay, okay, Anya," said the astrologer. "We get it. Nice show."

"No, I see him right now. I've never had this happen before."

"It's bad to stay in character offstage, sweetie," said one of the bead stringers. "It'll burn you out."

"No! I'm telling you the truth. At my show, this weird biker guy stood up and he said he was going to flick on my psychic switch. Suddenly, I could see Tom. And he's right here, right now. Can't you see him?"

The other bead stringer rolled her eyes dramatically. "I'm sure this entertains one and all at your shows." She scooped up a bunch of completed bracelets and put them into a box labeled "Tranquility Beads." The astrologer looked at the bracelets. "Sweetie, these sold better when they were 'Aura Balancers' and were from a commune, handmade by the 'Celestial Cooperative Collective.'"

"Listen to me!" Anya cried. "We've all been faking for so long. We've forgotten why we started in this business in the first place."

The astrologer looked up. "Nothing ever came of it. And, Anya, nothing, *nothing*, ever will."

Tom's ghost floated over to Anya and began whispering into her ear.

"Honey," said Tom, "you should ask her about the gym bag

in her closet. It's red. From the Australian women's swim team. The 1984 Los Angeles Olympics."

Anya repeated these words, and the astrologer froze.

"Wow," Anya went on, listening to Tom. "Inside the bag? Hostess Ho Hos? Ding Dongs? Twinkies? Why would she need so many? Oh, and there's a box of doughnuts."

The astrologer's jaw dropped. The chart in her lap fell to the floor. "Shut up!" she cried. "Just shut up. You don't know what you're talking about. You've never even been in my house or my closet. I find you rude. Rude."

The tarot-card guy piped up. "Anya, whatever you said, it's upsetting her. You're becoming a bore, sweetie. No one finds you funny, you know."

"Oh, no?" She listened to Tom's ghost some more and then turned to the tarot-card guy. "You were adopted. By an older couple, with teenaged kids. And you found out when you were grown up that the girl you thought was your older sister was really your mother! And your real father was her gym coach."

The tarot-card guy fainted onto the floor. As he fell, he flipped the coffee table over. Beads, bracelets, and several mugs of coffee spilled. A few crystal balls rolled off, and one of them made its way unnoticed into Anya's oversized purse.

The bead stringers looked at the tarot guy lying unconscious and wheezing. They looked at the astrologer, who was silent and quivering. They realized Anya was telling the truth.

Anya turned her gaze toward them, and they cowered. But she lost interest, rose, grabbed her purse, and went to the door. At the threshold, she paused.

"Be very careful what you wish for, my friends," she said. "It just might come true."

CHAPTER 6

Crystal Ball

Anya went out into the night, realizing her relationship with her fake psychic comrades was over. She made her way back to her apartment. Tom's ghost floated with her.

"Being dead is great," he said. "My prostate doesn't hurt anymore. I'm not sure I even have a body. I feel wonderful."

"Tom, this is weird. I miss you so much. I just want to hold you and kiss you, but there's nothing to grab hold of. I'm having a hard time with this."

"It's okay, baby. I'm here. Watching over you. Everything's fine. You have nothing to worry about." He disappeared.

Anya arrived back at her apartment and was greeted at the door by one of her overweight cats. Another was eating from a bowl labeled "Fluffy." Yet another was lounging on the vintage La-Z-Boy chair. Anya shooed it off and collapsed, exhausted.

Then she saw it. Across the room. The figure of a woman at the window, peering out. She was dressed in antique-looking clothes.

"Who are you?" Anya cried.

The figure turned to her and reached out her hand, but then dissolved away.

Anya shuddered. She reclined into the La-Z-Boy. On the floor in front of her chair was her electric footbath. She switched it on and kicked off her boots. It had a little waterfall built in, and the babbling sound was soothing. She reached for a box of long wooden matches on the side table and lit a strawberry-scented candle. She slowly lowered her feet one at a time into the hot water. She grabbed a box of incense, found a stick labeled "Purification Pine," which she positioned in an incense burner and lit, and fanned the fumes nervously in all directions. Satisfied, she eased back and took a deep breath. The room was peaceful and dark, illuminated only by the flickering candle and the orange glow of the incense's burning tip.

Suddenly, a breeze gusted through an open window, causing the set of crystals hanging there to tinkle. It was a pleasant sound, one Anya had heard many times before. But now, in her agitated state, it startled her. Seeking distraction, she reached down into her purse to retrieve a local tabloid newspaper she remembered putting in there. As she felt around for it, her fingers came upon a hard glassy sphere. A crystal ball. She held it up, admired it for a moment before realizing it was from the Celestial Cooperative Collective, and put it on the side table.

She flipped through the paper, and when she got to the back pages, she noticed a classified ad for a telephone psychic: "Mama Cleo's Psychic Friends Hotline." She felt the urge to call, so she grabbed her phone and dialed.

It was answered by a blonde college girl of about eighteen, wearing a phone headset, sitting on a bed in a dorm room, painting her toenails while talking. She spoke with a pretend Jamaican accent. She grabbed a cue card and read from it.

"Ha-lo, my dear! This is Mama Nostradamus, God-gifted spiritual counselor, soul-mate reuniter, and lottery-number blessings-bringer. Welcome, welcome, welcome."

"Hi," said Anya. "I've got a problem."

"What's your name, love?"

"Anya. Anya Dreamchaser."

"And your age, sweetie-love-mahn?"

"Fifty-three."

Going through a stack of binders on her bed—with labels like "Looking for Mister Right: Women" and "Excited White Guys"—the phone psychic chose one called "Middle-aged Crisis: Female."

"Is this actually Mama Cleo?" asked Anya, peering at the newspaper ad.

"No, my name is Mama Nostradamus. Mama Cleo is in a consult with another pilgrim. The main switchboard—er, *tabernacle* transferred your call to me. Don't you worry, sweetie-love. Me and Mama Cleo, we been working together for over forty years. Now, what's the trouble?"

"I'm being visited by my dead husband."

The phone psychic tossed aside the "Women in Crisis" binder and grabbed another one called "Bereaved Widow."

"Wait, sweetie-love," she said, "Mama Nostradamus sees all. I can see a man. With a wedding band."

"Yeah. My dead husband. Tom."

"He's in a better place now."

"But it's really hard to deal with. He's freaking me out. What am I supposed to do?"

"Do you have a plastic bag?"

"Yes. In the kitchen."

"Good. Put the ghost of your husband in the bag. Mail it to Mama Cleo's Psychic Hotline, and we can ghost-bust him."

"It's a human soul! I can't put it in a bag."

"Well, sweetie, do you suspect that your husband's ghost may be having an affair?"

"What?"

"Just a minute, sweetie. I mean, we must find your spirit guide. Yes. To get you through this crisis."

"Spirit guide?"

"Spirit guide, my sweet." By this point, the Jamaican accent was totally gone. "What we'll do is get you one of Mama Cleo's Intra-Dimensional Ectoplasmic Convecting Earth-Light Spheres."

"Spheres?"

"Well, a ball, really. Made of glass."

"You're trying to sell me a crystal ball?"

"You look into them, and they show you the way. You find your path through the crystal ball. Or you can get them to snow when you shake them."

"A crystal ball will solve my problem?"

"It's the only way to find your path. Then you'll stop seeing the dead guy and his new lover."

"What are you talking about? And I already have a crystal ball, Mama. It's sitting right here beside me. This is ridiculous. I think we're done."

"Wait. Do you have access to a live chicken?"

Anya hung up in disgust. She tossed the newspaper to the table, but it missed and dropped to the floor. Sighing, she rose and stepped out of the hot water, onto a towel, and then into a pair of pink bunny slippers. "Find my path through the crystal ball, eh?" she muttered, sarcastically.

Suddenly, one of her cats jumped onto the side table. It tilted, causing the crystal ball to roll off and onto the floor. It came to rest on the newspaper, right over an advertisement for bus excursions to the First Nations casino: "Dice 'n' Dinner Tours." The ball acted like a magnifying glass through which Anya suddenly noticed the ad, enlarged and slightly distorted.

"Find my path through the crystal ball," Anya muttered to herself, wondering if maybe this was no accident. Maybe this was a signpost pointing the way. She liked the idea of treating herself to some gambling. It would be a welcome distraction, and she might even win something. With her new powers, maybe her good-luck charms would actually work. Maybe she would win big. Through the glass, she read the phone number and proceeded to book herself onto the Dice 'n' Dinner bus package leaving the next morning.

CHAPTER 7

This Is My Church

Ralph gazed out the window at the city lights. Everything seemed different now. It was like the universe had thrown down the gauntlet. The Ouija board wasn't working, but he was still determined to gain psychic powers, by hook or by crook. Restlessness overtook him. He decided to go for a walk and get some air.

He headed downtown, toward the banking district. Soon, he was in front of the building where he worked. It seemed oddly peaceful. He gazed up at the steel and glass tower. The spattering of lighted windows looked like a constellation of stars.

He walked over to a decorative pool in the plaza out front. As he peered into it, a reflection passed over the murky surface of the water. It appeared to be the figure of a man pushing a shopping cart. Ralph looked up, but no one was there. Suddenly, an unusual-looking poster on a nearby lamppost caught his eye. He walked over to it. It said: "Looking for spiritual answers? Find them with the Circle of Isis."

Spiritual answers? It might be worth a try, he decided. He checked the address. It was in the old part of downtown where the buildings were antique and the streets were narrow. It wasn't far. When he arrived there, he saw that it was an old warehouse. At the basement entrance, there was a weathered sign painted with gold letters: "Welcome to the Circle of Isis." He walked down the crumbling cement stairs, gripping the cold, metal-pole railing.

The door was open. He went in and saw about two dozen people milling around and taking seats in a big circle of chairs. The room was a decent size, with a number of windows at grade level. The floors were bleached oak, and there were mirrors and wooden rails along the wall, leftover from its former days as a dance studio. The room was dimly lit with candles and two hollow stone tiki heads with flames burning within, creating an eerie orange glow from their eyes, noses, and mouths. One was perched on a dusty old upright piano, which looked like it hadn't been played in years.

He walked into the gathering timidly. He felt awkward, but right away he was approached by a friendly, prepossessing blonde woman who had clearly benefitted from good-quality plastic surgery. She was wearing silver bracelets and necklaces, one with a topaz amulet. She approached with warmth and confidence, like he was an old friend.

"Hi there," she said. "I don't think I've seen you here before. And why would that be?"

"Because I haven't been here before," Ralph replied.

"That you *know* of."

"Well, yeah. That I know of."

"Let's get to know each other so you don't feel like you're here without a friend. I'm Heather. I'm a Healing Daughter. My stone is topaz, so sometimes I get called 'Topaz,' but that's only on journey nights. Now, do you have a name?"

"Er, yes. I do. I'm—"

Heather cut him off. "I see your cuff links are hematite. Is that your stone?"

"Well, they are mine."

"Hmm, you're very possessive, aren't you? Well, everyone's welcome here, whether you can remember being here before or not. Let me introduce you to everyone."

"Look," said Ralph, suddenly feeling trepidation. "Maybe I should just—"

"Everyone," Heather called out, "this is our new friend. He's very chatty. I think you'll like him. His stone is hematite!"

"Welcome, Hematite," said the group, in unison.

"Listen," Ralph protested. "Just to set things straight—"

"Now, Hematite," said Heather. "I know you'd probably love to talk all evening, but we really must be seated when our Dark Mage joins the circle. His name changes every solstice. Right now he's named after … oh, what is it? It's an herb or a tea or a coffee or something."

She pulled Ralph down into a chair. Suddenly, a voice in the distance began to speak. It was a deep male voice with a slight lisp: "What circle is this that calls to the higher powers?"

"The circle of the goddess Isis," everyone replied.

"And what do you give to the goddess to summon her presence?"

"We give good, good, good vibrations. And harmonies."

From the darkness, a figure stepped into the center of the circle. He was a tallish man with dark hair tied in a ponytail. He was dressed in a floor-length bathrobe.

"Welcome the mage of the goddess," chanted the group. "Welcome, Luwak!"

Ralph raised an eyebrow.

"Luwak, Dark Mage," said Heather. "We have a newcomer. He is Hematite."

"Welcome, Hematite," Luwak replied.

Several didgeridoos were produced and passed around the group. People began blowing into the instruments. It was a very loud sound and a strange one. Heather handed Ralph a wicker basket.

"Here," she said. "You're going to need one of these. They're from Guatemala. Handmade. The people down there are so uncomplicated and wonderful. We could learn a thing or two from them."

"Really?" said Ralph.

"Oh yes. They make these baskets with their own hands. They put their hands right on the basket!"

Ralph scratched his head. The didgeridoo music stopped, and Luwak began to speak.

"I come to you to spread the divine essence of the goddess. Her strength is made new in me. We draw our energy from the Church of Isis, the Earth Mother."

Silence fell as Luwak reached behind him and grabbed the handle of a red Radio Flyer wagon. He pulled it into view. It contained what appeared to be a tarp and a bag of potting soil. The wheels squeaked slightly as he positioned it in the center of the gathering. He stood over it.

"Together, we take covenant with the goddess in her temple."

Everyone held up their wicker baskets.

"From her tears, we draw water."

Everyone held up bottles of water and shook them.

"From her sighs, we have wind."

Everyone held up paper fans and began fanning each other.

"From her core, we draw fire."

Everyone produced stick candles and lit them.

"And from her body, we have our church."

Luwak fell to his knees. As the glow from the candles illuminated the area, it became clear that what was in his wagon wasn't a tarp; it was an inflatable child's wading pool. He spread it out on the floor and attached an electric air pump. He switched it on. Slowly, the pool began to inflate.

"Hear the roar of Isis as she gives breath to the holy pool with her spirit."

A few minutes went by. The thing was taking a long time to blow up. Impatient murmurs came from the gathering.

"We're nearly there," he proclaimed. "Give it another minute."

It took five more long minutes, during which everyone stared awkwardly, listening to the hissing. Finally, he disconnected the pump and emptied the bag of potting soil into the pool.

"Goddess, hear us," he said, kneeling down to pray. "We bring to your arms a poor tormented and demented soul." He looked at Ralph. "Kneel, Hematite, and join me in celebration of the goddess!"

Reluctantly, Ralph knelt down, opposite Luwak. They both leaned over the soil-filled pool.

"Celebrate, Hematite!" Luwak cried. "Consecrate yourself with the Church of the Earth Mother, Isis! Repeat after me." He grabbed handfuls of soil. "This is my church!"

"This is my church," said Ralph, puzzled. He grabbed some soil.

"Consecrate yourself, Hematite," Luwak cried, rubbing soil on his own face. "This is my church!"

Ralph was too embarrassed to get up and walk out, so he went along with it. He rubbed soil on his own face. "This is my church," he muttered.

"The goddess can't hear you!"

"This is my church," said Ralph, louder. The others began emptying their bottles of water into the pool, making mud.

Luwak rubbed some into his hair, yelling, "This is my church!"

Ralph scooped a tiny amount of mud and put it into his hair. "This is my church."

"Don't be afraid, Hematite!" cried Luwak. "It's not something the cat crapped out. It's the Church of the Goddess. Now it's your church too! Tell me it's your church." Luwak daubed Ralph's face with mud.

"This is my church!" Ralph yelped, slapping mud onto Luwak's face.

"This is my church!" Luwak responded, splashing Ralph with a wave of mud. Ralph splashed back. Luwak grabbed him by the collar. They wrestled. Luwak forced Ralph's face down into the mud. "This is my church!" Luwak cried.

Ralph struggled and broke free. He spat out mouthfuls of mud. Gasping for air, he collapsed into Luwak's arms and began to sob loudly: "This … is … my … church!"

The group stood around watching and smiling. Ralph wept convulsively in Luwak's arms. Luwak rocked him gently and then looked up and sniffed the air. "Coffee's ready."

CHAPTER 8

Loose Threads

After cleaning himself off, Ralph went to the kitchen for coffee. He peered out a window looking onto a little courtyard and garden. Everyone was milling around, speaking with approval about his initiation. Luwak handed him a mug.

"Here. This should help calm your nerves." Ralph took it gratefully and grabbed some fresh homemade cookies, which were cooling on a nearby cookie sheet.

"Thanks, man."

Luwak peered kindly at Ralph. "Thanks, *person*," he admonished. "We of the New Age don't approve of gender, Hematite."

"New Age? I thought the worship of Isis was an ancient religion." He munched on one of the cookies.

"It is, Hematite. It is a very ancient religion dating back to the Egyptians and the Mayans."

They were joined by Heather, who was nibbling at the edge of a cookie. She pointed to the one Ralph was chewing on. "I'd go easy on those, Hematite."

Ralph finished his cookie and started on a second. "Egyptians and Mayans?" he queried. "But those cultures were thousands of years apart—"

Luwak interrupted. "Ah, you'll learn. We don't let facts

interfere with our faith. That's what makes us New Age. We just *know* it's right. We don't need to understand it."

Ralph looked puzzled. "There's no underlying theology? No rational study of belief? No learned discourse?" He reached for another cookie. "Mmm. These are good."

"No," Luwak replied. "We simply know we're right because we know we're right."

"And we love nature," chimed Heather. "Especially trees. It's the Druid tradition. We believe in trees."

"I'm having a hard time making sense of what you're saying," Ralph protested.

"Why do you need your beliefs to make sense, Hematite?" said Heather. "Isn't it enough that they are certain?"

"The physical world is damaged by the flagrant domination of the logical," added Luwak. "That's why we must look to the spirit realm for our answers."

Ralph rubbed his eyes. He was growing tired and woozy. He popped another cookie into his mouth. "Well, actually, that's why I came here," he said. "I want to have a spiritual experience."

"What do you mean, Hematite?" Luwak asked.

Ralph began to laugh nervously as he started into yet another cookie. "I, uh, went to see a psychic show. Expecting to laugh. I mean, it's hokum, right? But then, my buddy, a guy I've known for years—he … he knew things about people. He talked to the dead. I want to do it too."

"Well, you've come to the right place," said Luwak. "You will have a broadband, high-speed connection to the spirit realm. All of us Isisarians go on a vision quest to find our spirit guides."

"Spirit guide?" Ralph stammered groggily, with his mouth full of cookie. "Vision quest?"

"Like the Lotus Eaters of ancient Africa and the shaman of the Navajo, we eat the mind-altering sacred mushrooms of the Primal Wood of the Earth Mother. It takes us on our journey. We find our spirit guide on that journey."

"We find it's easier," Heather added, "to eat magic mushrooms when they're baked into cookies. Shouldn't really eat more than one."

"Magic mushrooms?" cried Ralph, blinking and shaking his head. "These cookies are spiked?"

Luwak gently guided Ralph up the stairs and out the back door, into the dark garden. "Enjoy your journey, Hematite. When you see your spirit guide, embrace it, and it will lead you on your quest."

"My spirit guide," said Ralph, wobbling and twitching.

Heather and Luwak stepped back into the doorway.

"Welcome to your new life, Hematite," Luwak declared. "Your new way of being."

The door closed. Ralph was alone. He trembled and wheezed. He staggered out a gate at the back of the courtyard into an alley. He managed to get to the end of the alley and onto the street. Luwak's voice echoed in his head: *Welcome to your new life, Hematite. Your new way of being.* Ralph pulled off his tie and tossed it.

After what seemed like an hours-long journey that really was only a few city blocks, he came to the entrance of a park. It was dotted with old trees and winding paths lit by wrought-iron lamps. In the distance, he saw an illuminated pool with a fountain. He staggered toward it, still hearing Luwak's voice in his head: *When you see your spirit guide, embrace it, and it will lead you on your quest.*

Ralph stumbled toward the fountain, peeling off his jacket. Now the mushrooms had really kicked in. His legs felt like jelly, and everything seemed distorted. He peered into the darkness, muttering to himself: "Spirit guide … must find spirit guide … I definitely need a guide for all this."

In the distance, he heard a sound. It was the squeaky wheels of a shopping cart. It grew louder and louder, like a chorus of angels, until a distant figure emerged from around the bend. It was Spud. He trundled into view, and Ralph could see his cart was full of stuff and he was wearing an aluminum-foil hat. He was pausing here and there to pick up rocks. As Ralph stumbled toward him, Spud looked up. They made eye contact. Spud was clutching an armful of hematite.

"Get away!" Spud cried. "These are my walnuts. Mine. My treasure of walnuts. Black diamonds of the park to be harvested. Go black-diamond prospecting somewhere else. Try James Bay."

Ralph was confused. He wondered if this strange man was really there or whether he was just a figment of his mushroom-spiked imagination. Suddenly, Ralph began to laugh uncontrollably. His knees gave out, and he fell over, convulsing with glee on the grass.

"You're a crazy man!" shouted Spud.

Ralph looked up and smiled. "Hi," he said dreamily. He stared at Spud for a moment and then turned his gaze sideways where he saw the fountain again. He realized it was not far away. To his drugged mind, it looked like an oasis, a welcoming paradise where he should go in search of a spirit guide.

He managed to get to his feet, though he swayed back and forth like he was going to fall any second. "Spirit guide!" he slurred. He staggered to the fountain. After twenty arduous paces, with Spud following behind, he reached the fountain pool. He removed his trousers and stepped into the water. Spud wheeled over and picked up the trousers, inspected them, and then stashed them in his cart.

"I wouldn't go in there," said Spud. "Crazy people crap in it. It's like coffee in there."

Stoned and heedless, Ralph began wading around in the fountain. "Spirit guide," he mumbled. "I need a guide."

His eyes spinning with the effects of the mushrooms, he peered into the pool, which was illuminated by underwater lights. There were flecks of dirt, dead flies, and mosquito larvae. Suddenly, he spotted something that interested him. It was a worm wriggle-swimming through the water.

Again, he recalled Luwak's voice: *"When you see your spirit guide, embrace it, and it will lead you on your quest."* Ralph cupped his hands and caught the wriggler. He raised it to his face. "Hello," he said gently. "I'm Hematite. You're going to lead me on my quest."

Spud, watching this and shaking his head, began muttering to himself: "That's the problem with the city. Too many crazies in the parks. Humph."

Ralph stepped out of the pool, his bare legs dripping with water. He looked at Spud's cart and noticed an empty whiskey bottle in it. He asked for it. Spud obliged. Ralph slid the worm into the bottle and scooped up some of the brackish, stinking water, which would be its new home. He screwed the cap on tight.

"Thanks," he said. "I couldn't carry my spirit guide around in my hands."

Spud nodded. Worry came over his face. "You can't walk around in your bare legs like that," he said. "I know; believe me. The Pants Nazis will be all over you." He pulled a garment from his shopping cart. "Here. I was gonna save this for good, but you need it more than me." He draped Ralph with a yellow, fluffy, much-too-small bathrobe with "World's Best Mom" embroidered on the pockets.

"Pants Nazis," mumbled Ralph.

"You'll blend right in now," said Spud. "Everyone has a bathrobe. Everyone has a mother!"

Ralph rubbed his hand across the fluffy lapel. "Mother," he said dreamily.

"And here. You'll need one of these. They stop the brain rays the big diamond cartels use to make you buy useless stones!" Spud took several old frozen TV dinners from his cart. He peeled off the aluminum lids and twisted them together into a makeshift cap. He put it on Ralph's head. "There. Now, what is it you put in the bottle, anyhow?"

Ralph showed him. "S'my spirit guide, man. I'm on a vision quest. It's gonna lead me." A tone of awe came into his voice. "It's an eel."

"Hmm," said Spud, skeptically. "Let me see that." He took the bottle and scrutinized its contents. "Well, I dunno how to tell you, son, but that ain't no eel. It's a flatworm. From all the crap in the pool."

"Flatworm?"

"Flatworm. Hookworm. Tapeworm. Son, your spirit guide is a bowel parasite. The public health nurse showed me one once. Comes from other people's crap. Just what guidance were you expecting to find there? You'll get nothing of value from crap."

Ralph peered into the bottle, muttering: "Nurse ..."

Spud rummaged through his cart and pulled out a handful of hematite stones. "Now these," he said, "these are your answer, son. Park diamonds. Diamonds the size of walnuts. That's where your answers are. Wealth beyond imagining. You don't need to buy diamonds when you can pick them off the ground. Black diamonds. Hematite."

Ralph looked at the rocks and started laughing uncontrollably. His legs turned to rubber, and he fell onto the grass.

"You okay, son?"

Ralph lay there giggling. Spud picked him up and leveraged his sagging body into the cart. Ralph nestled himself into the basket, grabbed his whiskey bottle, and held it close to his chest. Spud began wheeling him along the park path. "Now," he said, "let me show you where you can get more of those spirit guides. Fresh ones!"

"No way," Ralph replied. "One spirit guide is enough for me. I'm not going to be disloyal."

"Humph," muttered Spud, shaking his head.

They rolled along in silence for a while. Then Ralph started thinking out loud: "So, if the dead can be spoken to, that means there are souls. It's just science. And who knows what else? Angels? God?"

"And therefore devils?"

"Devils?" said Ralph, clutching his bottle to his chest protectively.

"Devils. I see 'em. Mind, they mostly take human form. Bankers. Lawyers. Business guys. Pants Nazis. Now, for the average person to talk effectively with the dearly departed, you have to approach it scientifically. You don't need a fraud telephone psychic."

"Frauds ..." sputtered Ralph.

Spud rummaged around in his cart. He pulled out a roll of duct tape. "I'm gonna give you something to protect you from the devils."

Ralph touched the aluminum cap on his head. "More foil?" he queried. "Or a silver bullet? Garlic?"

"No," said Spud, fishing something else out of his cart. "The one thing those money devils can't bear. The one thing they'll run screaming from if you make them so much as look at it, even for a moment." He passed Ralph a hand mirror. "Themselves."

Ralph looked into it. Seeing his drugged, disheveled image, he began screaming a high-pitched falsetto scream.

CHAPTER 9

Hell's Tartan

Gregory prayed feverishly until the Saturday morning sun rose. All he felt was guilt. He decided to pay a visit to his childhood church. He left a note for Leanne and tiptoed out of the apartment. After a short walk, he arrived at Saint Bernard's of the Water.

It was an old stone building. The steeple penetrated the sky, drawing the eyes heavenward. It wasn't an altogether peaceful sight, though. With its weathered green copper cladding and fierce, decaying gargoyles, the imposing spike seemed to inspire fear as much as anything else. Below it was the carillon, an ancient multibelled musical instrument Gregory remembered from when he was an altar boy. He used to sneak up the tower to watch the church organist beat the large wooden pegs with his fists to play those bells, producing a terrible music.

It had been a decade and a half since Gregory had set foot in this place. Now, here he was, walking up the front stairs, approaching the door through which he would make his spiritual homecoming.

Inside the church, a figure in a black robe slowly trundled down the center aisle. His pink balding head was shaved clean, and his face was gaunt, with thin lips and a pug nose. His priest's collar seemed a little too tight, and his eyes were frightfully dark and round, like two black buttons on an elevator to hell.

He walked past some elderly ladies kneeling in prayer. Behind them was a stained-glass window depicting a male saint rescuing animals from a flood. It bore the inscription "Saint Bernard of the Water."

As he reached the altar, he paused and looked up reverentially at a life-sized statue of Christ on the cross. He smiled in adoration. Then he took a deep breath and swooped down on a scruffy homeless man sound asleep in the front pew. He grabbed him by the collar and lifted him upright, causing him to gag for air. He dragged the poor soul to the door and threw him out.

Gregory witnessed this bizarre spectacle as he approached the church but decided to keep going regardless. He reached the door, entered, and gingerly walked down the aisle to take a seat at a pew. The place was now deserted. Gregory fell to his knees and began praying. He looked up at the statue and began speaking to it.

"Jesus?" he said. "I guess you know I've had a revelation. A doozie. Stuff I can't deny. I guess everything I learned about you when I was a kid is true."

The statue said nothing.

"Jesus, I have fallen into temptation. I have chased after silver, gold, and glittering prizes. I have wallowed in the garden of earthly delights. But now I need liberation. Maybe I should take a vow of poverty. Will that get me into heaven?" He took a breath. "Can you give me some kind of sign, Jesus? I've seen things that have changed my life. My friend talked to the dead."

The silence continued.

"Don't just stand there, Jesus; say something. Jesus?" He slowly approached the statue and deferentially touched its feet. Bursting into gentle sobs, he embraced its legs. Unfortunately, the screws anchoring it to the wall were coming loose. It fell, pinning him to the floor with a loud crash.

Suddenly, from out of the woodwork, the black-robed man appeared. "What do you think you're doing?" he bellowed, in a thick and furious Scottish accent. "You've ripped Christ off the cross! You've un-Jesused the church!"

Lying helpless beneath the statue, Gregory shuddered and whispered to himself, "Lord, no. Please. Not a Scotsman."

"What are you mumbling, laddie?"

"Father, I'm sorry. I came here to make a vow of poverty. And Jesus doesn't care. He fell on me. I'm having a spiritual crisis, and I need some help."

"You didn't need help un-Jesusing the church," retorted the Scotsman in disgust. "And what vow of poverty?"

"I haven't been to confession in years, Father. I think I could be in trouble with Jesus. I have fallen into the temptations of wealth and power. Now I want to make amends. I want to take a vow of poverty. But Jesus doesn't care."

"Care?" cried the Scotsman. "You worthless pig. It's just a statue. It's naught but chicken wire and a few pounds of plaster. What the devil is wrong with you? And besides, you can't handle a vow of poverty. Poverty's a *man's* game. You don't have the cojones for poverty." He spat aside in disgust. "You've no idea what decent, God-fearing poverty is all about."

"Yes I do. I could live in poverty and simplicity in a monastery. I'd wake up at five a.m. and pray for three hours. Then I'd have a simple breakfast with the other monks, then—"

"You self-indulgent twit!" screamed the Scotsman. "That's Club Med! That's Versailles, that is. Poverty is supposed to be bad, you ungrateful little sow. You won't sleep in a cushy monastery, oh no. You'll be sleeping outside in the street for a decade, and that's more than you deserve. Then maybe—maybe—Christ would take pity on your wretched, church-desecrating, un-Jesusing soul."

"But Father, what will be my shelter?"

"The wind. Your shelter will be the miserable, ceaseless wind."

"What will be my comfort?"

"The rain. The bitter, merciless rain."

"Where will I rest my head?"

"Stones will be your pillow! Cold, hard, unyielding stones. Stones that have no interest in your pain and will no hear of it."

"What will I eat?"

"Filth. Dirty, bowel-parasite-laden filth. You will eat nothing but filth because you are a dirty, dirty sinner who un-Jesused this church."

"But Father—"

"Don't 'But Father' me. You're not good enough for God. If God even noticed you enough to want to punish you, you should be grateful. It'll take many decades of cold poverty before you're fit for God's punishment. Aye, you make me vomit."

"Father, I think I'm barking up the wrong tree. I came here for comfort."

"You'll get no comfort here. What does it say out front? Does it say 'The Church of Wheedling and Mollycoddling?' No. It's the Church o' *Christ!* It's no a house of comforts."

"Father, I'm having difficulty breathing."

"You can't handle poverty, and you've ripped Jesus doon. Now I'm going to have to call the contractor to reattach the statue. And I'll be expecting you to pay for it."

Suddenly, footsteps could be heard approaching.

"Be quiet," whispered the Scotsman. He walked stealthily toward the footsteps. A priest was coming down the hall. The Scotsman quickly pulled off his own collar and removed his robe.

"Fitzie," said the priest to the Scotsman. "There's been a spill in the hallway outside my office. Would you mind mopping it up when you have a moment?"

"Yes, sir," replied the Scotsman, suddenly adopting a calm, deferential tone. "I certainly will."

The Scotsman walked down the hall toward the church's administrative offices. Some of the office doors had priests' nameplates on them, but he didn't stop at any of those. He went to one labeled "M. Fitzgibbon, Caretaker." He opened it. It was full of cleaning supplies. He took out a mop and bucket and went to clean up the spill, which turned out to be a dropped and smashed bottle of whiskey. After he finished, he looked around furtively and then put his collar and robe back on. He returned to Gregory, who was still pinned under the statue.

"Do you think you could get me out from under?" Gregory wheezed.

The Scotsman took hold of one of the statue's arms and heaved it up while Gregory pushed. With great effort, he wriggled free. He stood up and dusted himself off. He and the Scotsman examined the damage.

"I'm so sorry," said Gregory. "I'll pay for it."

"You can't afford to pay for what you did to Christ."

"Look, just tell me how much you want."

The Scotsman heaved a sigh of annoyed resignation and looked up at the cross where the statue had been. "It's gonna be at least five hundred."

"All right," said Gregory, "I'll write you a check. Payable to Saint Bernard's of the Water?"

"Don't be daft. Make it out to 'cash.' This must be kept quiet."

"Listen, Father, I understand what you said about taking a vow of poverty. Maybe you're right. Poverty's a man's game. But I really need to rejoin the church. Please. There's got to be something I can do to cleanse my soul."

The Scotsman's eyes widened as he looked disgustedly at Gregory. "What do you know about cleansing your soul? You come in here, wearing your fancy-shmancy suit and tie. You want to take a vow of poverty, but your suit alone could feed my homeless parishioners for a week."

"Why would they eat my suit?"

The Scotsman's face reddened even more than it already was. "My parishioners don't eat wool!" he screamed. "Have you naught but piddle for brains? What I meant was that for the cost of your fancy suit of clothes I could buy enough canned goods to feed my homeless for a week."

"I'm sorry, Father. Please tell me. What can I do? I want to help others. There must be a place for me in this church."

The Scotsman looked at him with slightly less contempt. His eyes narrowed, and he raised his hand to his chin. "Well, I suppose I could allow you to come along on my mission."

"What mission?"

"I'm leaving shortly to drive up to the First Nations reserve at Rama to distribute clothing to the needy. If you insist on pretending you're good enough for God, I'll let you ride with me. We'll meet around back. I'm driving the church bus. You can't miss it. And you should be grateful to ride in it."

In the parking lot out back, Gregory saw an old school bus painted a shiny cream, accented with a green stripe running under the windows. Below the stripe were the words "Saint Bernard's of the Water." The Scotsman loaded donated items—jeans, sweaters, and denim jackets—into garbage bags. There were also some toys, including a Frisbee, a soccer ball, and some old Hot Wheels.

CHAPTER 10

Best Friends Forever

The Saturday morning sun shone into Roger's bedroom through a crack in the curtains, casting a crisp line of light on the wall. He felt refreshed, ready for a road trip north with his best friend. He stretched his arms, rolled out of bed, and went to the kitchen to make coffee. Surveying the apartment, he was reminded once again that he lived alone—his tweed blazer was still draped over the chair and the empty glass of Nestlé's Quik was still in the sink waiting to be washed, a spoon standing in it, just as he'd left it the night before.

After a quick breakfast and a shower, he headed for the elevator with his knapsack over his shoulder and his gambling books under his arm. The underground parking garage where his candy-apple-red Mustang convertible waited was a low, dark, and filthy catacomb. The car was twelve years old, but it was the best he could afford. He kept it clean and in good repair. He hopped in and tossed his books onto the dashboard and his bag onto the backseat. The garage door opened, and the morning light blazed blindingly as he drove up the ramp. He put the top down.

Karl lived a short drive away, in an apartment on the ground floor of a stately Edwardian house on a leafy residential street. He had spent the previous evening there playing an online trivia game. Unfortunately, he was also plagued by random visions of various dead people. The incident at Anya's psychic demonstration had opened him up, leaving him susceptible to these unwelcome visitations. At one point, he saw a man whose face had been bloodied, possibly by a shotgun.

When Roger arrived, Karl was waiting at the curb. "Hey, Little Buddy," he said with a laugh, noticing the gambling books. "I see you're still obsessed with winning big."

"Darn right," said Roger.

"It doesn't work that way, dude," Karl replied. Then he paused for a moment in thought. "Well, there was that time about ten years ago. I was in a pub in England. They had this little slot machine at the bar. It paid off for me all night long. I bought drinks for everyone in the place."

"Really?"

"Yeah. I could feel the inner workings of the thing. I seemed to be able to influence the mechanism. It was weird."

"Dude, this is exactly what I'm talking about! They have slot machines at Rama. All you need to do is make friends with one of them, and we'll get our pot of gold."

"I don't know if I can make it happen again. I'm telling you, the psychic thing is not reliable or controllable. At least, it isn't for me."

"Don't say that. We need positive vibes. I need a cash infusion. I need to elevate my status. I want to *be* somebody. Then I can get a girl."

"This is about Sarah, isn't it?"

"Maybe."

"Dude, I know you insist on believing she's out of your league. But like I said, maybe she'll take you with her."

"Why would she be interested in me, a frustrated artist?"

"You're not *that* frustrated. You've got your weekly column. A lot of writers would give their eyeteeth for that. And you're working on your novel. You're doing okay. Your problem, dude, is in the courage department. There's no guaranteed way to move forward in this life. You want to plan everything. But you *can't* control the world."

"But I've worked so hard on my book. If I could just get published—"

"Dude, you're not listening. There's an old saying: 'Man plans; God laughs.' Have you heard that one?"

"No."

"Your fear of the unknown is your worst trait. Just ride the thread. Be of good cheer. You've got about as much backbone as a Kraft peanut-butter bear."

They drove along. The traffic was light, being a Saturday morning, and it thinned out even more as they headed north. The sun was rising higher, toasting their faces. After a few moments of silence, Roger broached a lighter subject.

"I wonder how they discovered Luwak coffee?"

"Must've been accidental."

"Must've been. I mean, who in his right mind would dig through cat poo looking for coffee beans?"

"Who digs through cat poo looking for *anything*?"

"Unless there were some veterinary reason for it."

Karl nodded.

"So, dude," said Roger, "what's up with your psychic thing?"

"What's up?"

"Yeah. I mean, you talked to the dead. Call me crazy, but I have some questions."

"Shoot."

"Okay. What's it like talking to the dead?"

"Boring, mostly."

"*Boring?*"

"They have different interests than us. They tend not to be up on current events. The dead are not particularly interesting."

"What do they look like?"

"Sometimes you can see them clearly, like a movie projection on the wall. Other times, you just kind of *know* they're there."

"Is it easy to talk to them?"

"Not really. Here's the thing: the dead are high."

"High? Like, high on drugs?"

"They've achieved nirvana or bliss or whatever. Heaven. No pain, no debts, no burdens, no questions, no mysteries. They laugh a lot. Laugh, and tell you they love you."

"The laughing dead!"

Karl paused. He noticed Roger had one hand on the steering wheel and was groping around in his knapsack with the other. Finally, he produced a long plastic-wrapped snack, which he tore open with his teeth.

"What are you eating?" asked Karl.

"Jerky. Want some?"

"Is it meat strips, or is it mechanically separated meat?"

"I don't know." Roger looked at the wrapper. "Doesn't say anything about mechanically separated meat. Says it 'may contain' a bunch of stuff."

"*May? May contain?*"

"Yeah. It says it may contain panda bear meat. Or stork. May contain stork. Mechanically separated stork meat. Or, stork meat by-products."

"All right, I'll have some."

"So, the dead say they love you?"

"Yeah. And forgive you. And then they say you should love and forgive too. And forgive yourself. Then they laugh some more. It's like talking to people who've just smoked a big fatty. But it's like you're calling from work. You know how irritating that is, being at work and talking to your stoned friends on the phone?"

"Yeah."

"Like that."

"Amazing!" Roger let out a cackle. "I'm going to make a note to myself: 'I no longer fear death.'" He laughed again. "A big fatty!"

"The jerky's not bad," said Karl.

"Yeah," said Roger, taking another bite and repositioning his hands on the steering wheel. They drove and took in the scenery, which was becoming increasingly rural and quite beautiful. After an idyllic few moments, Roger continued his line of questioning.

"So, dude, what about the future? Can you predict the future?"

"Yeah," said Karl. "But you don't always get it right. It's not like watching a video. Usually, you just see glimpses."

"Glimpses?"

"Yeah. And it's not one hundred percent reliable, or certain. I wish it were reliable. I bet the world wishes it were certain. The world craves certainties. People twist any little bit of psychic truth into complicated nonsense so it fits their other certainties. It's why most real psychics just lay low."

"Tell me about a glimpse you've had."

"I remember one time, back in the nineteen eighties, I had future-see of a really weird car."

"Future-see?"

"Yeah. It's my word. It isn't a vision, like in the movies. It's more like you're at a crowded mall with some friends, but you get separated and you can't find them because of the crowd. Then suddenly the crowd shifts, and for a moment, you can glimpse your friends at the far end of the mall. Future-see is like that."

"So the world is the crowd? And you only need the odd glimpse through it to know the direction you're going in?"

"Exactly. That's how I future-see."

"Cool!" Roger exclaimed. He handed Karl some more jerky. "So, tell me about this car you saw."

"It had circular seating in the front, like a luncheonette booth. Driver and passengers facing each other. Made no sense. Very futuristic, the future."

Roger pondered this. "You know," he said, "now that you mention it, you never seem quite as surprised as the rest of us when surprising things happen."

"Yeah. It's kind of like I'm in permanent déjà vu."

"What else have you seen?"

"One time, I saw an angel."

"Really?"

"It was amazing. I was talking to some dead people. And then, suddenly, this presence. I felt this warmth. This terrific, wonderful, warm love. Like a hand running across a harp that plays love instead of notes. It wanted you to know it was there. A vast loving presence that washed in and around and through everything." Karl paused for a second. "Man," he continued, "that jerky is good. Give me one more piece, then take it away."

"I don't know, dude."

"Just give me the jerky. I've lost control. It must have MSG in it."

Roger read the label. "Yeah. MSG. Dude, that's some cool metaphysics you're talking. Mind-altering stuff."

"Give me some jerky."

Roger handed him another piece.

"So this angel was headed back to wherever angels belong," Karl continued. "And at that moment, what your soul most craved was to grab hold and fly back along with it. Fly together. Home. Back to God, where you belong."

"Far out," said Roger, chewing.

CHAPTER 11

Looking Back

Roger and Karl continued their trek north, staying off the main highway, sticking to the scenic route. The terrain had become rugged, and the road snaked up, down, and around the green hills. The sky was blue and seemed like a theatrical backdrop against which God had introduced the few white puffy clouds floating by like cotton-candy sailboats.

As they turned a sharp corner at the bottom of a hill, a dark expression suddenly came over Karl's face. A shadow seemed to pass over the sun. "Ooh," he groaned. He was looking ahead about three hundred yards, at an old Victorian farmhouse.

"What, dude?"

"See that farmhouse up ahead?"

"Yeah."

"Great evil happened there."

The structure looked inhabited. There was a car in the driveway, along with a short yellow school bus. The house had a pretty design with a wraparound veranda and white pillars. The wall was red brick, and the wooden windows, each with nine rectangular glass panes, were original and in good condition. There were rusty lightning rods on the roof. The place looked okay to Roger, attractive, even, but Karl was on a different wavelength.

"How do you know?" Roger asked.

"Some places get imprinted by intense human experience," Karl explained. "Stored on the cosmic hard drive, I like to say. Some of those experiences were good; some were bad. This one was bad."

"What happened?"

Karl winced and looked away from the farmhouse as they drove past. "I'm not sure, and I don't want to delve into it. Let's talk about something else."

"C'mon; what did you see?" persisted Roger, like a dog who wouldn't let go of a bone.

"Let's just say domestic violence and leave it at that."

"What kind of domestic violence?"

"Let it go, Little Buddy."

"Cosmic hard drive," Roger chuckled, trying to sweeten the tone of the conversation. "And you're tapping into it."

"Yeah," said Karl, relaxing a bit as they rounded the corner and left the ancient crime scene behind. "It's like having a pair of goggles that pick up more than what other people see. And just 'cause they can't see it, doesn't mean it's not there. Not of much use most of the time, though."

"You know," said Roger, "this whole psychic thing might disturb me a lot more if you weren't so matter-of-fact about it."

"As it should be, Little Buddy. As it should be."

Noon approached, and they began to feel hungry. They kept their eyes open for someplace to eat. They drove down a steep incline with a lake at the bottom and came upon a small conglomeration of buildings. There was an old gas station with an Esso sign hanging from two rusting chains, a general store with a post office, and at the water's edge, an old building with a red roof and a sign saying "Victory Restaurant." It looked a bit shoddy but serviceable enough, under the circumstances.

"What about this place?" said Roger, squinting to read the sign. "It's called 'Victory.' Looks like it's been here since World War I."

"Or at least the last time it was cleaned was VE Day," quipped Karl. "It'll have to do. I'm starving."

They pulled into the parking lot. Apart from a mint-green, snail-back trailer sitting off to the side that looked like it hadn't been towed in ages (although it was not decrepit enough to preclude the possibility that someone might actually be living in it), there was only one vehicle in the lot: a dilapidated beige 1970s pickup truck. Its payload contained an old metal gas can, some loose lumber, and a wooden box that they hoped contained tools rather than a severed human head. There was also a cardboard box full of empty liquor bottles. Roger wondered what unfortunate soul was forced to drive a truck like this. Karl already had a dark inkling.

Inside, there was a lunch counter from the 1950s with round, chrome-edged stools upholstered in red vinyl. There were several tables and a few booths along the windowed wall facing the lake. The place was deserted except for a waitress who looked a bit frightful, though not unattractive, with her long, black, Goth-like hair and a silver bull ring pierced clean through her nose, in one nostril and out the other.

There was only one customer: a grizzled man in his late fifties. His hair was bushy and greasy and nearly silver, like mercury. His complexion had an unhealthy, shiny red glow. His bulbous nose was florid with gin pocks. His mouth ran straight across the bottom of his face, with lips so taught and thin they were difficult even to see. When they parted, his yellowed, battered tusks came into view, and they seemed to be permanently gritted into a snarl. He was by no means sober.

Roger and Karl avoided the booth beside him and sat down two over. The waitress came. She had earbuds shoved into her ears but somehow was able to carry on a conversation.

"Hi, guys," she said. "What can I get you?"

"I'll have the club sandwich and a coffee, please," said Karl.

"Same for me," said Roger. He turned to Karl. "Do you think they have Luwak here?"

"No. At least, not the store-bought kind."

Karl looked over at the grizzled man and suddenly got a glazed look in his eyes. His expression turned to revulsion and then horror.

Roger noticed and leaned in close. "You're doing it again, aren't you? You have that weird look."

"Yeah," grunted Karl. "I'm seeing stuff from that guy's past life. At least, I think it's past-life stuff."

The waitress brought the coffees and sandwiches.

"Wow," said Roger, taking a bite and deciding it wasn't half bad. "What do people think when you tell them? About their past lives?"

"They never listen. And when they do listen, it's only to screw around. Either burst into tears that they've never been loved or get all huffy and blame me that they weren't Cleopatra before. No matter what, mayhem ensues. So I say nothing."

"Can you see my past life?"

"Aw, Little Buddy. What makes you think you aren't brand-spanking new?"

As they ate their sandwiches, the grizzled man drained the last drop out of an empty beer bottle, which had a lipstick-stained straw stuck in it. He then scooped up a loose-change tip that had been left by the previous customer. He realized the waitress was watching him. She reached under the counter and pulled out a flyswatter.

Karl got a strange, distressed look on his face again. "What are you seeing?" asked Roger. Before he could answer, the grizzled man noticed Karl looking at him. He staggered to his feet and shuffled menacingly toward their table.

"No worries, dude," said Roger, frightened. "My buddy is psychic. He's seeing your past life."

"Shhh!" said Karl, annoyed.

The grizzled man plunked himself down beside Roger and faced Karl. "Go ahead, Kreskin, tell me what you see. Then maybe you can bend some spoons."

The waitress muttered, "No spoon bending."

Karl gave Roger a dirty look. He was peeved at being put on the spot, especially by this drunken cauldron of rage. Deciding to go with the flow, he looked the poor haggard soul in the eye.

"Okay," said Karl. "I'm seeing trench warfare. World War I." The look of horror returned to his face.

"What are you talking about?" the grizzled man thundered. "Trench warfare?" It wasn't clear whether he was angry or merely drunk. Roger grew anxious and realized he should have kept his mouth shut. Suddenly, the grizzled man's face lit up, and he cracked a pathetic smile. His dentition resembled that of a badly carved jack-o'-lantern. "I was a soldier? In the trenches?"

"You're lying facedown in the mud," Karl continued. "The British army. Yes. A soldier about to die in the warm, wet mud. And the reason the mud is warm and wet is because it's not just mud; it's the guts of one of your dead comrades. You died facedown in your friend's intestines."

"I was a war hero!" cried the grizzled man. He turned to the waitress. "Hey! I gave my life for my country! Yeah. Once, I was a hero. Me!" He buried his face in his hands and sobbed quietly. Roger put a comforting arm around him and muttered to Karl, "See what good you can do with your powers, dude?"

"Little Buddy, the only thing I've given this guy is a fresh grievance to shout when he's drunk."

"You drunk again?" the waitress asked.

"I drink every day, and you know that. But these boys have shown me I'm made of better stuff. I can get off my crappy welfare check and get a big fat veteran's pension. From England. I suffered for those Limey frogs. They owe me." He rose to his feet and gesticulated to the empty room. "I'm a veteran, and I'm entitled to a pension!"

Karl and Roger decided they'd better leave. They threw money on the table and discreetly headed for the door. The grizzled man began frothing at the mouth. "The English owe me. Owe me big. They're gonna pay my tab."

The waitress lost interest and went back to her work. Roger and Karl jumped into the Mustang and roared away. The grizzled man collapsed at his table and started singing "London Bridge Is Falling Down."

The waitress went toward the kitchen and looked in at the cook through the serving window. "Ya know," she said, "I never like to say nothing on account of I don't want people to be jealous, but I called one of them psychic lines once. And you'll never guess who *I* was in my past life. I'll give ya a hint: I broke men's hearts, and Elizabeth Taylor played me in the movie."

Out in the car, Roger turned to Karl. "Wow. World War I. Trenches. That's heavy."

"Yeah," Karl replied, glancing nervously back at the Victory sign as they drove away. "But I'm not always sure."

"Not sure it was true?"

"Oh Lord, no. It was true. But it's possible I was reading someone else in the immediate area. I get the signals crossed, you know."

"Pretty awful for whoever lived it, though."

"Yeah," agreed Karl, glancing tenderly at Roger. "Just be grateful you are brand-spanking new."

CHAPTER 12

Chariots of the Gods

Spud wheeled Ralph along under the Saturday dawn sun, down a road on the fringes of the now-deserted banking district. Ralph was wearing a duct-tape necklace from which dangled the hand mirror. It was resting against his chest facing outward. He clutched his bottled spirit guide in one hand. He was still in thrall to the mushroom gods.

Spud held forth on his spiritual and theological theories: "And so one might say the Bible is the Magna Carta of human imagination," he said, peering at Ralph, who was smiling, with a drop of spittle running down the corner of his mouth.

"Far out," said Ralph.

"Then of course there's the wisdom of Socrates, and the meditations of Marcus Aurelius. Let me see now, I used to know this by heart, having taught it so many times and to some of the stupidest jarheads to ever ride through officers' training on a military scholarship."

"Taught? You … you were a teacher?" Ralph said in wonder, slobbering. A loose thread hung from the sleeve of his bathrobe. He pulled at it.

"Teacher? No. Professor. Quantum mechanics, particle physics, telemetry." He shuddered. "Oh, that darned telemetry project! Now, Marcus Aurelius believed that many things in this world can be changed and improved. But many things are predestined. Woven into the fabric of the universe. Of course, like any fabric, you'll find that once in a while, you get caught on a loose thread. What happens to a garment when you pick at a loose thread?"

"It unravels?"

"Exactly. It unravels. And if people insist on picking at the loose threads of the fabric of their little piece of the universe, they become unraveled. When you find a loose thread, just let it alone. Or follow it along. But don't try to unravel it yourself." He paused to adjust his aluminum-foil hat. He looked at Ralph's hat and adjusted it as well.

"'*Oh, we know what God wants us to do,*'" cried Spud sarcastically. "'*Oh, our holy book is the right one.' 'Oh, call now, our psychics are waiting.' 'Oh, twelve easy steps to fixing everything.' 'Oh, take another expensive course and there will be a place for you on the mother ship.' 'Oh, we've invented a brand-new ancient religion made out of herbal tea and specialty coffees.'* Humph. They have a coffee now that's made out of cat crap."

"It's called Luwak," said Ralph. "It's very good."

"Nothing good comes out of crap."

Ralph pulled the last of the thread out of his bathrobe sleeve. The cuff fell off.

"Gotta learn to see the threads, son," said Spud. "Without feeling that you have to pick at them."

They trundled on into the morning light. It was becoming warmer and rather pleasant. They reached a valley with a road leading out of the city. It was lush, green, and peaceful.

Spud began to chant softly: "In mercy, hear thy children's cry. Oh, Bread of Life, thou in thy word hast said, who feeds on me shall never die! Father, give us this day our daily bread."

Ralph was looking into the mirror, turning it clockwise and counterclockwise, trying to see the image of himself from different angles. Disgusted, he held the mirror out over the edge of the shopping cart and shook it. He looked back into it. He shook it again.

Spud stopped his chanting and spoke. "Now, I was sort of a lapsed Protestant until it all happened. You know, kept Christmas and went to funerals, but that was about all. Never gave it a second thought, really."

"Never gave what a second thought?"

"You know. *It*. All of it. The fabric. The nonmaterial part of the universe. Spirit. 'The Force.' Not until that day."

"What happened?"

"Well, it was at the height of the depths of the Cold War. Before your time."

"Commies?"

Spud nodded. "And if the Reds were gonna wipe out humanity, we were gonna be darn sure we wiped out humanity first!"

"Reds," Ralph echoed.

"We were looking for something, *anything*, that could give us an advantage. You wouldn't believe some of the technologies. Trained dolphins. Microfilm cameras hidden in tie clips. Deadly weapons hidden in children's toys."

Ralph seemed astonished. "Tonkas? Slinkies?" He took a deep breath. "Hot Wheels?"

"No. Never Slinkies. And because of my work in physics, I was often asked to review projects for the military. Mostly it was gadgetry. Then one day …"

Spud began recounting a tale from his past. He described being in a military office, underground, in a deep bunker designed to be safe even in nuclear war. It was the late seventies, and he was young and clean-cut, wearing a white lab coat.

He remembered it like it was yesterday: he was standing in front of an army-issue desk made of green metal. Seated at it was Captain Buford Mayhew. There were papers, reports, and drawings flung all over the desktop. There was a paperweight made of hematite, and a chipped coffee mug emblazoned with

'Visit Beautiful Sedona.' Beside it was a bowl of walnuts in the shell.

"Look, Professor," said Mayhew to Spud angrily. "I know you're the foremost quantum physicist in the world, so I'm gonna let your outburst pass."

"I can't be expected to take data like this seriously," Spud retorted. "It's an insult. There's no way this could happen. The woman in charge is clearly a liar, or a madwoman."

"Now, Major Wilson is not a liar."

"Madwoman then. Mad as a hatter."

Major Mary Wilson, an attractive black woman in a US Air Force uniform, was sitting next to Spud. "*I'm in the room!*" she cried indignantly.

"Madwoman in the room," said Spud. "Or, possibly, liar."

"I don't have to put up with this," said Major Wilson. "I really don't." She stood up to leave.

"Now, Major, er, Mary …" Mayhew said. "Let's just all calm down."

She paused and then reluctantly sat back down.

Mayhew stared angrily at Spud. "Professor. That will do. You've seen the results. We know it worked. We'd just like to understand how. We need you to give us a theoretical model of why it worked. With some certainty."

"Certainty?" Spud said in disbelief. He pointed at Major Wilson. "I'm certain that she is a liar. Or …"

"Don't say it," Mayhew cautioned.

"Look," said Spud. "I've seen the reports written by your so-called 'psychics.' And I've seen the photographs from the satellite. What I want to know is: how could those men, in a basement in Colorado, have drawn the details of a Siberian missile silo in the Kamchatka Peninsula before we saw the telemetry? I want to know." He paused for a second. "The dates must have been altered, or maybe the …"

"We've verified that the drawings were completed twelve weeks before the telemetry," said Mayhew.

"They didn't need the telemetry," chimed Major Wilson.

"They didn't want the telemetry," Mayhew said.

"They can't have done it without the telemetry!" Spud protested.

"No telemetry," said Mayhew.

"No telemetry," said Major Wilson.

"Madwoman!" cried Spud.

"If you call me that again, I'm leaving this meeting."

Spud covered his mouth, but it slipped out. "Madwoman."

"That's it," said Major Wilson in disgust. She stormed out.

A short, awkward silence followed.

"Are you happy now?" Mayhew cried. "You've just offended one of the finest investigative scientists we have!"

"Or madwoman."

Enraged, Mayhew stood and leaned across the desk. He looked Spud in the eye. "I don't give a rat's rump that you can't wrap your mind around the realities of this project," he cried, his Texas accent becoming more intense. "It's hard for me too, hard like trying to pass solids after a week of drinking hard liquor. In all my years in military intelligence, I've seen strange things. A lot of it hard to swallow, at first. The pictures of the Commie slave camps, the report on global warming, the dead Roswell alien in a freezer in Area 51 ..."

"Area 51?" said Spud, surprised. "There are Martians?"

"There's one less. Where do you think all these great technological leaps of the last few years came from? In this era, with no Edisons, no da Vincis, no Wright brothers, and yet we spew out brilliant inventions. From where?"

Spud realized he was hearing the truth. His mouth fell open.

"It fell from the sky!" said Mayhew. "We're getting people used to it, slowly. We've even been working with a Hollywood TV producer to spoon-feed the public new ideas. Maybe you've heard of him? Gene Roddenberry. Anyway, there's a lot more to the universe than your classroom. And this psychic project is just one more thing you never knew about before. Get used to it. Accept it. Or it will make you crazy."

"It's for real? Real? *Real?*"

"As real as tits on a fat man. And just as sometimes-not-pretty."

Spud began to quiver. "If it's all true, then my life has been incorrect. And this ... this changes everything."

As Spud finished his story, he looked at Ralph and began to stare wistfully into space.

"Star Trek is real?" Ralph said.

"That's not the point," snapped Spud. "The point is my life changed that day. I left my study of physics and threw myself into parapsychology, for which the university and my wife both eventually turfed me. I lost my job, my money, my home." He paused and tapped his forehead with his finger. "But I still got the noodle."

"Star Trek is real!"

"Would you get off the Star Trek thing?"

"Space, the final frontier!"

"Would you stop with that?"

The magic mushrooms had worn off enough that Ralph was now able to walk. He trudged alongside the shopping cart as they neared a grassy embankment. Spud looked at him and spoke. "Our journey together is coming to an end, son. It's time to move to the next step."

"Where am I going?"

"I can't say where you're going next, son, but I think your ride will be along shortly. Find your thread. And don't pick at it!"

He turned and began wheeling his cart back toward town, leaving Ralph standing at the side of the road, in his yellow bathrobe, clutching his bottle, still without trousers. Ralph stuck out his thumb.

CHAPTER 13

Chance Meetings

The Scotsman pulled the sun visor down as he drove the church bus into the Saturday morning glare, out of the city and north to Rama to minister to his needy flock. Sitting behind him was Gregory, who glanced up and noticed a cricket bat in a Velcro sling hanging within reach of the driver's seat. On the cricket bat, in black marker, were written the words "Corrective Implement." The Scotsman looked in the rearview mirror and noticed Gregory eyeing it.

"Don't even think about fussing with my educational tools, you!"

Gregory looked at him quizzically. "What is it?"

"It's just what it says. If you don't behave, you get the corrective implement across the calves. If you're really, really out of control, you get it to the buttock. And if you're in some sort of street-drug, Protestant-induced frenzy, a tap of that to the gonads will settle you right down."

"You don't actually use that? On human beings? You're kidding, right?"

The Scotsman heaved a knowing sigh. "In order to learn, you need consequence for your actions. Reward for good, decent, Christian behavior, such as learning to use the potty. And severe physical pain for undesirable, un-Godly behavior, such as—well, you hardly need a lesson from me on bad behavior, Mister 'Oh, I'll just pull Christ down off the cross because my life has no meaning.' Ach." He spat contemptuously onto the bus floor. "It's how you learn. There's a science to it. It's called 'behavior modification.' Very cutting-edge. But then, as you've noticed, I'm a very progressive thinker."

"Who do you modify exactly?"

"It works on the mongoloids and pinheads in special-education class at church. Keeps them from touching themselves."

"Pinheads?"

"Aye. It's a medical term. It means they've heads like pins."

A few awkward moments passed. Then, up ahead, on the side of the road, something came into view. It was a bus pulled over on the shoulder. There were orange traffic cones set out. A uniformed driver stood waving his arms crossways above his head. On the side of the bus were the words "Dice 'n' Dinner."

"What's this?" said the Scotsman. "Looks like we've a bus in distress. I suppose I should stop. It might be an opportunity to do some good. Besides, I can always use another fare." He pulled over and stopped behind the traffic cones. Gregory watched as the Scotsman got out and walked over to the other bus driver. They began talking. A few elderly passengers emerged and joined the conversation. It looked like they were haggling with the Scotsman, who appeared to be getting angry. Gregory reached for the cricket bat, removed it from its sling, and hid it underneath his seat.

Finally, things calmed down. The Scotsman moved into position in front of the church bus as the casino-bound passengers lined up. They were mostly seniors. As they boarded, each one handed ten dollars to the Scotsman.

One of the passengers fumbled for a long time in her oversized hemp purse before finding her ten dollars. Gregory was busy trying to keep the cricket bat from sliding out from under the seat, so it would be a while before he noticed that this woman was Anya Dreamchaser.

Anya walked down the aisle toward the back of the bus, which by now was chockablock. There was only one seat left, next to a kindly looking man with a gray, military-style brush cut. It was Captain Mayhew. They smiled at each other as she sat down.

"Sure is a nice day to go to the casino," Mayhew said good-naturedly. He was wearing a black T-shirt and a waist-length khaki jacket.

"Sure is," Anya replied.

"Yup. Too bad the bus broke down. Lucky we got a backup. We shouldn't have to pay extra for it though. Still, I expect the money will go to the good works of this church."

"Good works," agreed Anya.

Mayhew looked toward the front of the bus. "This bus driver priest seems a little excitable."

The Scotsman was driving with one hand on the wheel; with the other, he was poking around with frustration at the empty cricket bat sling.

"Oh, yes," said Anya. "His face is really red."

"Now," said Mayhew, "you're a little young to be on a bus full of retirees."

"Oh," Anya said with a laugh. "I just wanted to get to the casino, and the 'Dice 'n' Dinner' bus seemed like the best way. Well, the best way I could afford. So, you're retired, eh? Tell me, what did you do?"

"I was a captain in the US Air Force."

"Really? My. Did you see any action? Oops, I mean, that's none of my business. I shouldn't have asked you that." Anya blushed and looked demurely away.

"It's okay," said Mayhew, reassuringly. "I did two tours of duty in Vietnam."

"That must have been awful."

"It was. After Vietnam, I joined the Psych Ops. Sort of an intelligence unit. Fought the Cold War. I was stationed in Colorado. Colorado in those days was a lot less frightening than Vietnam. But in some ways, it was more disturbing."

As Anya listened, her hand accidentally brushed against the bare skin of Mayhew's wrist. As their two fleshes made contact, her eyes widened. A channel opened, and she began seeing a vision of his past. It was vivid. She could see him presiding over three army psychics who were poring over maps of Siberia. On the table next to the maps was a box of doughnuts.

"Colorado was more disturbing?" she queried. "How so?"

"I probably shouldn't talk about it." He produced a box of doughnuts. "I brought these. Want one?"

"Oh," she said. "What kind?"

"Well, there's a raised chocolate. And a Hawaiian. I don't much care for a Hawaiian doughnut." He made a face as if he were having his teeth pulled without anesthetic. "The little colored worms cause me consternation. In Vietnam, I suffered from a bowel parasite. Dirty water. And those multicolored worms on a Hawaiian doughnut tend to remind me of that troubled, troubled episode I wish to forget. I'd sooner think about napalm than what happened to my hindquarters when that bum critter worked its mischief."

Anya's mouth dropped open and stayed that way for a second. "Oh," she said finally. "I don't blame you. I'm not a fan of Hawaiian doughnuts either."

"Thanks for saying that, ma'am. You seem to understand me in ways most people don't."

"And I definitely prefer raised chocolate."

"God bless you, ma'am. You know, I think you can judge people by their doughnuts. I'm a raised chocolate man, and I don't care who knows it."

"What about plain glazed?"

"That's a whole 'nother story. There's some dignity to a plain glazed, I'll grant you that. A quiet dignity. However, I see it more as a historical doughnut. A sort of proto-doughnut, a tribute to the formative years of the doughnut industry. But don't get me started. It's complicated, the way I see it."

"Okay," said Anya. "And listen, if you want to talk about

what you did in Colorado, I won't laugh at you. After what's been happening to me recently, I'm ready to believe anything."

"Well," said Mayhew, "it was a fascinating time, I must say. I was working with psychic folks. They were doing something called 'remote viewing.' Very strange. But it seemed to work."

"Are *you* psychic?"

"No, ma'am. My job was strictly administration. And motivation. I operated the reward system, and occasionally the corrective implement."

"Reward system?"

"Yes, ma'am. It was doughnut-based. I hung doughnuts from strings, above the psychics. Just out of reach. When they gave me some good intelligence, I'd lower the doughnuts. The strings were on a pulley system. It was quite something. I engineered it myself."

"Really?"

"Yeah. But I'll tell you—they were a persnickety bunch, those psychics. Kept complaining about the coffee. Said it tasted like crap. But I told 'em it came from the NASA laboratories. Same stuff the astronauts get. Mind you, sometimes NASA had problems with the processing."

"How was it processed?"

"I'm afraid that's classified."

"What were the psychics looking for?"

"Russian missile silos."

"Could they see them?"

"Yes, ma'am. On the Kamchatka Peninsula. And it was before we saw the telemetry."

At the front of the bus, Gregory was talking to the Scotsman. "I've got a question for you. If God is benevolent and all-powerful, why is there evil?"

"What are you driving at?" retorted the Scotsman. "Are you suggesting there's something wrong with God?" He groped around in vain for the cricket bat.

Up ahead in the distance, at the side of the road, the figure of a hitchhiker came into view. He was dressed in what appeared to be a cape. As they got nearer, they could see it wasn't a cape but a bathrobe—yellow, fluffy, ill-fitting, and missing a part of one sleeve.

"What have we here?" said the Scotsman. "There's a man hitchhiking in a bathrobe."

"Hey!" Gregory cried. "I know that guy. We have to stop."

"Well, if he's a friend of yours, I guess he's a friend of mine," said the Scotsman. "And I can always use another fare."

The bus slowed to a stop several yards past Ralph. The doors swung open. Gregory leaped out.

"Ralph! What are you doing here?"

"Gregory?"

"Yeah! What happened to you? Where are your trousers? And what's in the bottle?"

Ralph looked down at his bare legs and mouthed the words "Pants Nazis" to himself.

"I've been on a walkabout, man," said Ralph. "My mind has been blown."

The Scotsman watched from the bus. He had located his cricket bat, which he cradled ominously.

"I've been on a journey too," said Gregory. "Back to the church. It's been weird." He glanced nervously back at the bus. "I even found—well, not a mentor or friend or anything. More like a spirit guide."

Ralph smiled and reached into the oversized pockets of his bathrobe. He pulled out a handful of dirt and smeared it across his forehead. "This is my church, man." He raised his bottle. "And this, this is my spirit guide."

Gregory looked at the bottle, peering into its murky contents. "Um, I think it got away. All I can see is a flatworm."

"Nah, man, this is him. My personal spirit guide." He gently opened the bottle.

Just then, the Scotsman approached, carrying the cricket bat.

"Ach, what's going on?" he cried, crinkling his nose in disgust. "Did you soil yourself? Have you been digging around in an outhouse?"

"Easy, man, it's my spirit guide," said Ralph, recorking the bottle protectively.

"That does it. Time for the corrective implement." The Scotsman deftly snatched the bottle from Ralph and set it down on the ground. "Spirit guide, indeed. Some people have peculiar notions about the spirit world. Dirty sinner."

Before anyone could stop him, the Scotsman positioned himself in front of the bottle and raised the cricket bat like a golf club. "Fore!" he cried, swinging powerfully, making a solid connection with the bottle. It went flying, miraculously unbroken, and disappeared over a high embankment. On the other side was a service road along which a pickup truck marked "City Parks and Recreation" happened to be driving, carrying a load of loose manure. The bottle landed in it and lay nestled there unnoticed as the truck continued its journey toward downtown.

"That was my spirit guide!" Ralph cried. "What did you do that for?"

"Enough with your blasphemy," growled the Scotsman. "There'll be no bottles of crap on my bus. Nothing of value comes from crap."

"That's not true. We drank coffee that came from crap. Cat crap from Indonesia. It's called Luwak. Eight bucks a cup."

The Scotsman slapped him on the calves with the cricket bat.

"Ow!" Ralph cried.

"Do you want a tap of this to the 'nads?" bellowed the Scotsman, brandishing the bat. "Do you? Because that's where you're headed, my son. Keep talking, and you get a correction between your legs, I promise you. Now, if you want a ride in my bus, you will stop your filthy un-Christian behavior, and you will come on board, sit down, and keep quiet. And the fare is twenty dollars."

"I have no money. I haven't even got pants."

The Scotsman raised his cricket bat in anger, but Gregory quickly grasped and immobilized it. "Wait," he said. "I'll pay for him." He pulled out a twenty-dollar bill and handed it to the Scotsman, who became somewhat mollified.

"All right, into the bus then. And watch yourselves."

They all climbed aboard. The Scotsman strapped his cricket bat back into place in the Velcro sling and then sat down behind the wheel. He checked his mirrors and merged back onto the highway.

CHAPTER 14

The Visionary

Roger scowled as his Mustang suddenly lost power. He pulled off to the side of the road as the engine gave a final sputter. He looked down at the gas gauge.

"You've got to be kidding," said Karl. "We ran out of gas?"

"I know, dude. The warning light never came on. I was going to fill up in the next town. I thought I had a while to go yet. The light must be broken. Man, this sucks."

They sat in silence for a moment, looking around, realizing they were in the middle of nowhere. Up ahead, maybe a quarter mile, they saw what looked to be a side road or a driveway. They got out of the car and began walking toward it.

As they got closer, they saw it was the entrance to a trailer park. There was an archway made of galvanized metal tubing, which formed crude letters spelling "Diamond Park." They passed under and followed the desolate gravel road. Finally, they came upon a mobile home.

It hardly looked like a trailer. The wheels were hidden by a large wooden deck, big enough to accommodate a picnic table. There was a carved wooden bear in the corner with a straw hat on its head. It looked friendly.

There was an allotment for a yard, but instead of grass, it was covered with stones—river rocks, rounded and smooth. In the middle was perched a lawnmower, spray-painted gold, mounted on a small boulder.

"Wow," said Karl. "What is this place?"

Before Roger could comment, the screen door of the trailer opened and a portly, red-cheeked old man with a snow-white beard poked his head out. With his red T-shirt and gold wire-rimmed spectacles, he looked a bit like Santa Clause on summer vacation.

"Afternoon, fellers," he said good-naturedly, his hillbilly accent tinged with surprise. "What can I do for you?"

"We've run out of gas," Roger replied.

"Good gravy. There ain't no fillin' stations nearby; I'll tell you that. If you have a jerry can, I can siphon some out of my truck."

"I'm afraid I don't have a can."

"Well then, I'll see what I can find. I might have an empty bottle or two inside. You fellers come in and have a seat while I get a hose."

"Thanks. That's very kind."

They went into the trailer. There was a living room with an old mustard-colored sofa facing a large television. On one of the wood-paneled walls, there was an enormous buck's head. There was a black woodstove off in one corner, next to which was sitting a pair of good-quality rubber boots. About ten feet away was the kitchen with a small table and some wooden chairs. The aroma of coffee wafted out.

The old man gestured to the sofa and told the guys to sit down. He went into the kitchen and began rummaging around. He retrieved a pair of old whiskey bottles.

"These'll do," he said as he put them on the counter. Then came a loud meow as a black cat jumped up and began sniffing them.

"No, Fluffy! There's nothing here for you today. Get down." He turned to the guys. "You fellers want a coffee while I get the gas?"

"Sure, thanks," said Roger. Karl looked apprehensive.

The old man poured two cups and brought them out.

"This is newfangled stuff I'm trying. It's called Luwak."

"Really?" said Roger with a smile. "That's funny—we just tried some yesterday. We liked it."

He and Karl raised their mugs and took sips.

"It's really expensive," the old man continued, "*if* you buy it in a store. Fluffy, get outta there."

Roger and Karl looked at the cat and immediately spit-sprayed the coffee out of their mouths.

"I think you only do that with wine, boys."

"Sorry," said Roger. "I think we're a little carsick."

The old man fetched some paper towels, and Roger wiped up the mess. "It's very good," said Roger. "I just don't feel well."

"I'm still working on the recipe. Maybe it's a bit strong."

He took the bottles and went out to his truck. Karl and Roger looked at each other.

"You okay?" Karl asked.

"Yeah. You?"

"Yeah."

"This is weird."

"If he comes back with a bag of quick lime and asks for our dental records, we make a run for it, okay?"

They sat in silence for a while. Roger noticed an unusual-looking framed picture on the wall. It was a pencil drawing of a long, wheeled vehicle. It seemed like a car, but it looked like a rocket. The nose was twice as long as the passenger cabin.

"Check that out," said Roger. "What a cool craft. Looks like something out of *The Thunderbirds*."

"Maybe this dude is an inventor or something," Karl replied.

The screen door opened, and the old man walked in. He saw the guys eyeing the drawing.

"I see you fellers have noticed my pride and joy. It'll drive straight into a brick wall at sixty mile an hour. I call it the Sedona

Crashmobile. I invented it when I was living down there in the desert. I wish someone had listened to me. It would have saved many lives."

"You designed this?" Roger asked.

"I most certainly did. But no one was interested. No one. Back in 1961, I tried to show it to President Kennedy. He was visiting Ottawa. Him and Jackie were there. Guests of honor at a state dinner. By gum, I took those blueprints and tried to show the president, but the guards wouldn't let me in. Instead, they arrested me. I spent the night in jail. Then they took me to see some sawbones, a psychiatrist or some darn fool thing like that. I didn't need no doctor. *He* couldn't do anything with my plans."

"Wow," said Roger.

"Let me show them to you," said the old man as he reached behind the woodstove and retrieved a dusty cardboard tube. He spread the blueprints out on the coffee table. The nose-cone of the car was packed with sponge rubber and an elaborate system of springs.

"Amazing," said Roger.

"It would have saved many lives," said the old man, shaking his head wistfully as he gathered up the blueprints. Karl noticed a different drawing mixed in with the pile; it was a drawing of another car. It was round, with benches facing each other instead of seats. It looked like a luncheonette booth. He raised his eyebrow but kept his mouth shut.

"Well, fellers, there's two bottles of gasoline outside on the picnic table. That should get you to the next fillin' station."

"Thanks again," said Roger. "Can we give you some money?"

"Never you mind about money. We don't get many visitors here, and I'm happy to make your acquaintance."

The guys shook the old man's hand and went out to the deck. They grabbed the bottles and headed back to the car.

"What a nutcase," said Roger.

"Not a bad inventor though," Karl replied.

Chapter 15

Convergences

The church bus arrived at the casino. The entrance was crowned with a majestic octagonal tower of wood and stained glass depicting First Nations symbols: sky, water, moon, and stars. As the bus made its way toward it, the Scotsman suddenly stopped at a big blue charity drop box. He reached behind his seat, grabbed the garbage bags of clothes and toys, went out to the box, and tossed them in.

"What are you doing?" Gregory asked.

"Caring for my flock."

"Oh."

They reached the entrance. The Scotsman got out and positioned himself at the bottom of the bus steps. He stood there smiling and nodding affectionately as the seniors got off. They avoided making eye contact with him. One elderly woman had trouble getting her oxygen tank down, and the Scotsman, with a lit cigarette wedged in his teeth, gave her a hand.

Ralph exited the bus, having removed his ridiculous bathrobe in favor of more suitable clothing he had found on board—a caretaker's coverall with "Saint Bernard's of the Water Staff" on the back. At least it had pants. Gregory followed behind, keeping an eye on his friend, who was still a little unsteady from his mushroom trip.

Anya disembarked, and Ralph suddenly recognized her. "Hey, you're the bogus psychic we saw!" he blurted. "Well, you were bogus until Karl turned you on!"

Mayhew stepped up protectively. "And who might you be?"

"Name's Hematite, but my friends call me Ralph. And this is my friend Gregory. Who are you?"

"Captain Buford Mayhew, US Air Force, retired. What's all this about my friend here being a bogus psychic?"

Anya piped up. "Buford, there's something I should tell you." He looked at her with curiosity. "I used to do shows. Psychic shows. Mostly I was just faking it, but I wanted it to be real. Then last night, I did a show at the university, and suddenly it *was* real. This creepy guy in the audience stood up and starting talking to the dead. For real. Then he looked at me and said he was going to turn on my psychic switch. Suddenly I could see my dead husband. I could talk to him."

"I'd sure like to hear more about all this," said Mayhew.

Ralph scratched his head and interjected. "Wait a second. This is weird. Why are we all here together? Don't try to tell me it's a coincidence. No. I think something special is supposed to happen. This whole spiritual-world-psychic-meaning-of-life thing. Something brought us all together."

"It does seem uncanny," said Mayhew. "It reminds me of my time in the air force. I'm feeling the same strange undercurrents I used to feel in that basement in Colorado. An energy, like."

"I hate to say it, but you may be right," bellowed the Scotsman. "I did'na even know any of you. Not a man jack o' you. And now here we are, together. And I've heard such strange malarkey out of you people. Yet, truth be told, I've found it seductive. Like it was somehow meant to be that I'd get myself tangled up with a bunch of silly-asses. And I let myself get very tangled indeed."

"Tangled," Gregory agreed.

"Yeah," said Ralph. "Maybe our personal journeys are like the threads of a story line, and here they are meant to meet. On this day. At this time. In this place."

"At a palace of games of chance!" cried Anya. "People testing their fortunes." She reached into her purse and pulled out a handful of her gambling good-luck charms. "Well, boys, I don't know about you, but I'd say it's pretty obvious what it means. Fortunes are here to be made today."

"Of course!" cried Ralph. "Fortune! Fate wants to put wealth into our hands. Good old everyday wealth. Something tangible we can understand. Something we know we can believe in! I just wish Karl were here. With his psychic abilities. Man! We'd be scoring, for sure."

Just as he said those words, Roger and Karl pulled into the far end of the parking lot, unnoticed. They got out and walked toward the casino entrance. Karl turned to Roger. "Well, Little Buddy, here we are."

"Excellent," Roger replied. "You know, I just feel lucky today. Really pumped. Like today is supposed to happen. Are you getting into ooh-spooky-abracadabra-mysteries-of-the-universe mode?"

"Yeah. I've been psyching myself up for a while. And I gotta say, I do have this funny, nagging hunch."

"What?"

"Lives will be changed today. For the better. Marvelous changes."

"This is gonna be sweet!" Roger exclaimed. "We're going to be millionaires!"

Unaware of Roger and Karl, the church-bus gang went into the casino and got rolls of silver dollars. They took the closest available slot machines. Ralph sat at one called "Queen of the Nile"; it was decorated Egyptian-style with pyramids and the Sphinx. Gregory sat at one called "Lucky Matterhorn," which had an alpine theme of snowcapped mountains and a Saint Bernard wearing a rum keg around its neck. Mayhew sat at "Soldier of Fortune," which had cartoon images of mercenaries with guns and ammo belts. The Scotsman took "Creation's Bounty," with pictures of fruits and vegetables flowing out of a cornucopia. Anya sat down at "Crystal Ball," with its magical artwork depicting a psychic in a turban.

As they got ready to put in their first coins, Ralph glanced up. The crowd shifted, opening up a channel, and he caught a glimpse of Roger and Karl just outside the casino doors. He leaped up with excitement. "They're here!" he cried. Everyone looked, except the Scotsman, who was preoccupied with feeding coins into his machine. "Karl's gonna lead us to our bonanza!"

They all got up and started threading their way through the crowd. But as they did so, the channel closed just as suddenly as it had opened. They lost sight of Roger and Karl.

Roger and Karl didn't enter the casino. They stopped short of the doorway. There was a booth set up with local First Nations artists selling handmade arts and crafts. A colorful blanket had caught Roger's eye. It had a beautiful needlepoint design showing two lovers embracing in the sky, surrounded by stars.

The seller spoke to him. "It's called 'The True Lovers.' It is one of the constellations my people see in the night sky. The 'true lovers' will always be together and always be happy. I believe you people call that constellation 'Cassiopeia.'"

"I'll take it," said Roger. "I think the girl I'm going to give it to will really like it."

As the seller put the purchase into a bag, Karl stood looking at the casino door. He had a strange expression on his face. He seemed to be trying to figure something out.

Roger stepped toward him holding up the blanket. "This is cool, eh?" he said. "Man, if only true love was as easy to come by. Maybe after we win big, you can ask the stoned dead guys to guide me."

Suddenly, Roger noticed something hanging from the blanket. "There's a thread loose on this."

Karl's hand darted over and deftly grabbed it. "Don't," he said slowly, almost dazed. "Don't try to fix this yourself. You know what, Little Buddy? I just got this notion. Like, the crowd shifted. Grandma can fix this. Fix it right. I think we should go to Grandma's house right now. We can come back here later."

"Okay, dude. You're the abracadabra guy."

They turned and headed back to the car.

By the time the church-bus gang reached the doors, it was too late. They watched helplessly as Karl and Roger drove off.

"Where are they going?" Ralph cried. "They didn't even come in!"

"Hey," said Gregory. "Didn't Karl say they were going to visit his grandmother? I was there once. I'm sure I can find the way."

Everyone stood looking at each other. Anya started to watch an empty place off to one side. "It's embarrassing," she said. "But I must tell you that my husband's spirit is back. I'm trying to make sense of what he's saying, and, oh, I'm so new to this, but he is smiling. Laughing, even." Suddenly, she turned and looked at Mayhew. She tried to conceal a blush. "Ooh," she said, smiling. "I'll just go along with whatever you guys think is best. It feels right. And for this to happen at a house of chance—I'd say maybe fate has something special it wants to bestow on all of us."

The Scotsman piped up. "Ach, if we're all going to buy into this fate-fortune-predestined-voodoo, we may as well ride it all the way. Back to the bus it is, then."

Inside the casino, unbeknownst to any of the other travelers, were Sarah and Wanda. Wanda was at a blackjack table totally caught up in her game. Sarah stood next to her, looking bored, with several First Nations paintings under her arm. Her boredom turned to agitation when she glanced up and in the distance saw Roger and Karl outside the casino doors.

"Hey, it's Roger and Karl from The Labyrinth!" she cried, but Wanda was concentrating on the cards and didn't really hear. Sarah reached into her purse and pulled out two identical hotel room keys. She slipped one into Wanda's blouse pocket and then turned and rushed to the doors. When she got there, she saw

Roger and Karl driving away. Then she noticed the church-bus gang.

"Hey," she said. "You're the guys from The Labyrinth."

"Hey!" said Ralph. "How are you doing? Funny to see you anywhere but there."

"For the love of God, man," cried the Scotsman. "This is no time to be making whoopee with the girls from labyrinths or mazes or whatever hooley-booley you get up to."

"She's a friend," said Ralph. "And The Labyrinth, it's where we know her from, saw her last, where all this started." He turned to Sarah. "But imagine running into you."

"Yeah," said Sarah. "I never expected to run into you guys. And I just saw Roger and his buddy. They just drove away."

"I know," said Ralph. "We saw them too. We think they're headed for Karl's grandmother's place. It's not far. We're going to follow them. Something strange is happening. You want to tag along?"

"It's meant to be," said Anya.

"Well," said Sarah, hesitating. "Um, well … I guess so. I can leave my friend here for a while. We both have keys to our room. And I'd really like to talk to Roger about something."

"It's about the walnut goggles, isn't it?" said Ralph. "Well, it's actually *Karl* you should be talking to. Come on; we'll fill you in on the way."

As they crossed the parking lot toward the bus, Sarah looked back over her shoulder through the casino doors and glimpsed Wanda. She waved good-bye, but Wanda didn't see her. She had just sat down at "Creation's Bounty," the slot machine the Scotsman had been playing. She put a coin in, pulled the handle, and three walnuts came up. Lights flashed, and bells and whistles sounded.

CHAPTER 16

Ridin' the Thread

On board the church bus, the Scotsman was at the wheel barking abuse at Gregory, who was standing behind him giving directions. Sarah sat in the back with Ralph and Anya and Mayhew as they filled her in.

Karl and Roger were actually several miles behind, having stopped at a sewing shop called The Loose Thread to buy some presents for Grandma. So the bus was the first to arrive at her place.

It was a red-brick country house whose front garden was dotted with little ceramic statues—a gnome, an Egyptian cat, a Saint Bernard, a gypsy, a Scotsman playing pipes, and a Madonna.

The bus parked, and they all trooped up the front steps and gathered on the landing. They looked through the screen door and saw Grandma inside, gently moving to and fro on a rocking chair. She had sewing on her lap and was tugging at a thread. Gregory tapped on the door. Grandma came and looked out suspiciously.

"Hello!" said Gregory. "We're looking for Karl. We're friends of his. Good friends."

Grandma peered at him.

"I met you once before," Gregory continued. "Here, a couple of summers ago. Is Karl around? We're all good friends of his."

There was a little "click" as Grandma locked the screen door. "My," she said. "Good friends of Karl. Who are you all?"

"I'm Gregory. And this is another friend of Karl's. I don't think you've met him. Ralph."

"Yes," said Grandma. "You're the one that likes stones. Hematite?"

"Um, well, I guess," Ralph said. "Have we met before?"

"No. No, not at all."

"And this is Anya."

Grandma looked at Anya and then shifted her gaze to an empty place beside her. "I'm sorry about your loss, dear," she said, smiling gently.

"And this is Captain Buford Mayhew," continued Gregory. Then he looked at the Scotsman to introduce him but realized he didn't know his name.

"Good afternoon," said the Scotsman, stepping forward. "I'm Father Mandrill Fitzgibbon. In all honesty, I haven't actually met your grandson, though I look forward to that supposed pleasure."

"Oh my," said Grandma. "A Scotsman. I suppose you brought your bagpipes?"

"Well, now, as a matter of fact, I am a piper. And I do happen to have my pipes on the bus."

"We get a lot of rock musicians around here. On account of the casino and all."

"I'm no garage-band, long-haired rock-and-roller, miss. I'm a classical musician." He looked around at the incredulous faces. "What?" he cried indignantly. "Classical bagpipe. I'm a prize-winning classical piper."

"They give *prizes* for that?" Grandma asked.

"I won the Crystal Chalice at the Glengarry Highland Games."

"They give prizes for that! Do they give prizes for honking the horn of your bus, as well?"

An awkward silence followed. "You can wait around back,"

Grandma continued. "All of you." She turned to the Scotsman. "Please don't bring your pipes. I don't want the neighbors to see them."

As the gang turned to go, Grandma called out to Sarah, "Except you, dear. Why don't you sit down on the stoop, and I'll get you a nice cold soft drink. You just stay put and away from that bunch of sillies."

Sarah politely complied. The rest of the group went around back where they discovered a swimming pool in which was floating a very large Saint Bernard.

"Oh my dear Sweet Jesus Christ on the Cross!" cried the Scotsman. "There's a pony fallen in her pool!"

"Looks more like a Saint Bernard," said Ralph.

Grandma called out from a window. "Don't mind him. He's the neighbor's dog. He likes the water. He's not your concern."

"That dog is gonna drown," said Gregory. "With all that fur getting wet, it will go straight to the bottom. We should get him out of the water."

"Dogs can swim, dude," said Ralph. "Don't worry about it."

"But it must weigh two hundred pounds," said Gregory. "It's obese. This isn't natural."

Grandma shook her head and returned to Sarah on the front stoop, carrying a glass of Coca-Cola on ice and a small bowl of walnuts. She sat down beside her.

Suddenly, the crunching of tires on the gravel driveway announced the arrival of a shiny red Mustang with Roger at the wheel. His face lit up when he saw Sarah, who was smiling from her perch. He got out of the car and climbed up, carrying his blanket under his arm, with Karl two steps ahead.

"Oh, sweetie," Grandma said to Karl. "I'm so glad you are here!" She hugged and kissed him and then grabbed Roger and kissed him too. "I've put some lasagna in the oven this morning since you'd be bringing so many friends."

"How many are there?" asked Karl, with a knowing smirk on his face.

"Five around back, sweetie, fussing with the neighbor's dog in the pool. You should go talk some sense to them."

Roger turned to Karl: "How did she know there'd be people coming?"

"Grandma doesn't just ride the thread," Karl replied, tapping his temple to get his point across. "She sews with it."

"Then you can come in and see your nieces," Grandma continued. "My new lodgers have been teaching them some moves, and they are just as cute as anything."

"Musicians from the casino again?" said Karl.

"Yes, dear. These ones do Diana Ross and The Supremes. '*Love child, never quite as good ...*' Oh, it's been just so sweet listening to them practice. And you should see your nieces. But first, why don't you boys go do something about those addled chums of yours out back?"

Roger glanced aside at Sarah. "Hi," he whispered. "Fancy meeting you here."

"Hi," said Sarah, smiling.

"Listen," Roger continued. "There's something I need to talk to you about."

"Don't worry," said Sarah. "I heard what happened."

"You did?" he said, smiling with relief.

Grandma reached over to Roger's blanket and grabbed the loose thread. "Oh my," she said. "That will be needing a little attention, won't it? Leave it with me." She took the blanket and held the walnuts out. "Help yourself, dear, to tide you over until the lasagna is ready."

"Thanks," said Roger, taking one. He looked at Sarah. "Would you care for a walnut?"

"Sure."

He handed her one and noticed there was a happy face drawn on it.

"My nieces," said Karl. "They'll draw on anything that will hold still." He picked up a couple of the walnuts, held them to his eyes, and turned to Sarah. "Like looking at the world through a pair of walnut goggles, isn't it?"

"The ones with happy faces taste better," Grandma interjected. She turned to Karl and Roger. "Now go on, you two. Go around back and see to your friends. Sarah and I are having a chat."

She turned to Sarah. "Let's go inside. I'd like to talk to you about something." They went in and sat down. Grandma grabbed her sewing kit and started working the loose thread on Roger's blanket back into place.

"You seem like such a nice girl," said Grandma. "Nice, nice, nice. How on earth did you get tangled up with this bunch? Hold this, will you?" She handed Sarah the end of the loose thread.

"Well, I sort of know the guys from where I work, and, er—"

"So, you like Roger, do you? He's such a nice boy, that one. A nice boy. And he has a bright future, that's for sure. Brightest future of that bunch. A girl could do worse."

"How did you know? Yes, I actually do like him. I like him a lot. I've never told him, but I do."

"Well now, of course you do. You'd have to like a fellow an awful lot for a sensible girl like you to get on a strange bus with such a collection of strange folk." Grandma took the thread back from Sarah, and with a couple of stitches, the blanket was fixed.

"I never really thought about it," said Sarah, "but I guess I'm here because … because really, I guess I just wanted to be around him or with him. See him outside of work, you know? But I never knew I was doing that until just now."

"And a pretty thing like you, with a bright future of your own. Yup, you could do a lot worse than to tie up with Roger."

Grandma leaned over to the table next to her rocking chair and grabbed an embroidered pillow she had been working on for the past few days. She smiled at Sarah and resumed the job with amazing skill and precision. She reached into her basket, took a pair of scissors, and snipped a thread.

"It's all happening so fast," said Sarah. "It's hard to make sense out of all this."

"Some things just make less sense than others," said Grandma. "But in the long run, we really don't need to understand everything. Because as soon as you stop trying to understand things that can't be understood, they become so much easier to live with, if you see my point. That bunch out back don't know how to live with uncertainty."

"There are no certainties?"

"Just this." Grandma put down the scissors and handed Sarah the pillow. It had the letters "R" and "S" embroidered on it, clasped together in a lovers' knot. Surrounding them was the red outline of a heart. Sarah's mouth dropped open. Her eyes widened in wonder.

"It's for you," said Grandma. "I've always liked Roger. Now come on; we better go check on those addlepates in the backyard. Let's see who listened and who didn't, shall we? No more sewing. I can only tie up so many loose threads in one day."

CHAPTER 17

The Fabric of the Universe

When Roger and Karl got to the backyard, they found everyone in a mad struggle to get the Saint Bernard out of the pool. Gregory and Ralph were in the water trying to push the sopping beast up, while Anya and Mayhew were on shore tugging at its collar. The Scotsman was hurling abusive commands.

Karl shook his head in disgust and stepped onto the diving board. In silhouette against the setting sun his stature seemed to grow. Everyone stopped what they were doing. He looked down at Gregory and Ralph in the water.

"Guys!" Karl cried. "You just couldn't leave it, could you? You couldn't listen when I warned you, could you? And warn you, I most certainly did."

"But what you did changed everything," protested Gregory. "You ... you opened up a window. We've been looking for answers ever since."

"I don't have the answers. My psychic ability only lets me see the occasional thread of the fabric of the universe. And if we're lucky, it's a thread we can ride for a while and squeeze some good out of. But there's no owner's manual. My advice is to ride the thread, but don't try to untangle it."

"What are you talking about, man?" cried Ralph. "You gotta

give us something. Throw us a bone. Give us one answer even. One answer we can understand."

Karl sighed. "Okay, so what's the question?"

Gregory and Ralph both appeared ready to speak, but they realized they didn't actually know what the question was. Before anyone else could say anything, the Scotsman piped up.

"I have a question," he bellowed. "Are you people all daft? The dead, the past, the future, the meaning of life? It's all just clouds in your eight-dollar-a-cup, cat-crap coffee. And while you try to 'come to grips' with those clouds in said cat-crap coffee, there's a pony drowning in this pond!"

With that, the Scotsman joined Mayhew and Anya at the ledge of the pool and reached for the dog's collar, while Gregory and Ralph resumed pushing.

Suddenly, a little girl's voice called out from inside. "Grandma, where are you? We're ready to do our show for Uncle Karl!"

Music started up. It was the 1967 recording of The Supremes' song "The Happening." From the back door, three long, graceful gloved arms appeared. Then three much smaller arms poked out, also in gloves. Grandma's lodgers—three gorgeous young black women dressed as The Supremes circa 1967—danced out, followed by Karl's three little nieces, who were grinning from ear to ear. They were all wearing feather boas and Diana Ross wigs.

They danced their way around the pool, lip-synching to the music. As they went past, one of the nieces threw her boa around Sarah and Roger and tied it into a knot. They started laughing and dancing.

The struggle to rescue the Saint Bernard came to grief. The animal managed to pull Anya, Mayhew, and the Scotsman into the water. It then broke free and paddled to the pool steps, walked up, shook its enormous body, and went back to the neighbors' yard where it plopped itself happily down on the green grass and went to sleep.

The song and dance ended, and Grandma called for the backyard picnic tables to be set for dinner. She fetched towels and bathrobes. Everyone dried off, put his or her clothes in the dryer, and donned the robes, which were embroidered with "Sedona Healing Spa."

They all sat down and partook of the steaming lasagna. Gregory and Ralph and Anya told their tales. Roger was intrigued and surprised. Karl didn't seem surprised at all. The supper was congenial; there was laughter, and even the Scotsman was able to refrain from barking abuse long enough to enjoy it—sort of.

Once everyone was finished, and all the tales were told, the Scotsman reluctantly agreed to drive the gang back to the city. Karl decided to go along with them so Roger could be alone with Sarah. The gang boarded the bus, and Sarah and Roger headed for his Mustang. Everyone bid farewell. Grandma walked up the steps, went inside, and turned out the lights.

The bus drove off, leaving Roger and Sarah standing in the driveway under the black, starry sky. It was quiet, except for the faint sound of crickets.

"Crickets," said Roger. "Reminds me of up at the cottage. Sitting on the dock at night, looking at the moonbeams on the water."

"You can never catch them, you know."

"Moonbeams?"

"Yup. I tried once, up at my cottage. Swimming, trying to catch up. Can't be done."

"Wow. Where's your place?"

"North of Kingston. Bon Echo. The Mazinaw."

"Never heard of it."

"I love to sit on the dock too. Look out on the water. Plan my life."

"Really?" said Roger, intrigued. "Me too. How's your plan going?"

"Pretty good. How about yours?"

"Well, I'm behind schedule getting my novel published."

"You will. I really like your column."

"Thanks. But you know, I still don't feel like a somebody. I don't feel ready for love. Silly, huh?" He laughed to himself.

"I think we're always ready for love. All of us."

He suddenly saw his whole life flashing before his eyes, like he was drowning, but in a good way. He felt like throwing caution to the winds. He suddenly felt like he *was* somebody. Was he ready for love? He realized it didn't matter now. It never had.

"Hop in," he said, opening his car door. "Let's sit and look at the stars awhile." They wrapped themselves in the blanket. Sarah showed him the pillow Grandma had made.

"Wow!" said Roger.

"Can you believe this?"

"It's amazing. Now I see what Karl meant when he said his grandma doesn't just ride the thread; she sews with it."

"Do you know the constellations?" Sarah asked, pointing up at the stars. Her voice was warm and kindly. "There's Cassiopeia. And there's Scorpio, and there's Leo. Leo is the lion. See how you can trace his shape?"

As she raised her arm to point, Roger slid closer.

"Yeah," he said.

"Okay. Follow it down. That's the lion's back."

Roger squeezed closer still, looking up at the sky. "Wait a minute," he said. "Where's his head?"

"You've got to use your imagination."

"I'm trying to use my imagination, but I don't see his head. It's just some stars. Just a jumble. You want me to look at a jumble?"

He turned to her, and she turned to him. Their faces were inches apart.

"What are you talking about?" she asked.

"The universe looks like a jumble. A jumble of diamonds in a dark pond."

"I think it's like a big, beautiful fabric, sparkling with sequins. A fabric that we're part of. Like a tapestry."

"Maybe you're right. A big, beautiful needlepoint fabric, full of surprises. And sometimes …"

They spoke together in unison: "… you get caught on a loose thread."

They looked at each other in surprise.

"Sarah?"

"Yeah?"

"Do you think maybe I could kiss you or something?"

Sarah smiled. "Start with a kiss. The 'or something' might come later."

CHAPTER 18

Mugs and Bottles

The sun was rising red out of the mists that lay thick on the horizon. As the warm light came into Roger's apartment window, he noticed his coffee mug cast a shadow straight at him. Another Monday morning, back at work. He took a sip of the steaming brew. It wasn't quite as exquisite as Luwak, but it was rich and satisfying just the same. He looked out, reflecting on his good fortune. He thought of Sarah. He smiled and put the mug back down, and its shadow appeared again. He felt good inside, knowing there would be a phone call later today, either to her or from her, and they would talk and laugh and plan their next rendezvous.

He worked awhile. Then he made an expedition to the kitchen for more coffee. As he rose from his chair, a message from Karl popped up on his computer screen: "Future-see, dude. Call me."

Roger got his coffee and dialed the phone. "What's up?" he asked. "What are you seeing?"

"I'm seeing a golden future for you, my friend."

"Really? What's going to happen?"

"It's more of a feeling. Can't see anything too specific. Except for some shining happy people up at a cottage somewhere. Bon Echo maybe?"

"You've heard of that place? I never did, until Sarah told me she has a cottage up there."

"I used to go there as a kid," Karl replied. "I'm from Kingston, remember? Looks like you'll be spending some quality time there soon."

"Cool!"

"I'm also seeing Ralph's future. Wow. He's talking on a cell phone. Which is weird, because he's in the lotus position, in a yoga class. He's wearing a T-shirt with 'I'm a Believer' on it and a picture of the Roswell alien. He's tugging on a loose thread on his shirt."

"Dude, that *is* weird."

"Hold on—oh God, I'm seeing something different now. It's an old wooden sign saying 'Church of Saint Bernard of the Water Community Soup Kitchen.' Gregory's there."

"What's he doing?"

"He's using a beat-up aluminum ladle to dish out soup to the homeless. One of the homeless dudes is getting up to leave, and Gregory is spraying the chair with Lysol. Now he's scowling—he's discovered a piece of Silly String left behind. He's picking it up. He's throwing it in the trash can. But it's sticking to his hand."

"Again with the Silly String."

"There's someone standing behind him. It's the Scotsman. He's comforting some downtrodden guys sipping their soup. And his hand is resting on what looks like a cricket bat in a strange holster."

"That's bizarre."

"I'm seeing Anya and Mayhew now. They've set up a booth together at a Star Trek convention. There's a sign saying 'Area 51 Revealed.' Anya's blindfolded, and she's pointing out spots on a map. There's a bunch of Trekkies watching her, holding satellite photos. Now she's peeking out from her blindfold and … Mayhew is handing her a doughnut."

"A doughnut?"

"Yeah."

"I wonder what that's all about."

"I don't know, dude. Do you want to meet at The Labyrinth later? I think Sarah's working today."

"You read my mind. I told you I'd win big! See you there later. And if Gregory and Ralph show up, I guess I'll be getting myself a free Luwak."

Roger smiled and hung up. He took his coffee out to the balcony to get some air. He looked out at the western sky. Not far away, in the park, by the water fountain pool, a manure truck pulled to a stop. The driver got out and went across the street to get a coffee. In the truck's payload, nestled in the manure, was Ralph's bottled spirit guide. Suddenly, a dirty hand reached in and snatched it.

Spud put the bottle into his shopping cart. He trundled toward the fountain with the wheels squeaking. At the fountain, he stopped, opened the bottle, and returned the bowel parasite to its murky home. Then he went off into the sunrise.

As he pushed his cart, he began muttering to himself: *"Brewed, brewed in a cat's butt. The guy has a big meaning-of-life secret. Oh, the girl with the walnut eyes. The fake clairvoyant is made real, and the suits take journeys. One will un-Jesus his church and have a Scottish demon foisted upon him. Another will eat magic. The spirit guide is the worm ... or the madman? The fabric brings all threads together."*

He was being watched by several people who were gathered near the fountain, standing motionless, staring into space, wearing yellow bathrobes and no pants. Each cradled a bottle.

The End

EPILOGUE

My writing partner Steve Mueller and I completed a screenplay version of *Crystal Balls* in the spring of 2003. Steve passed away a few months later, so he never heard the radio drama of one of the scenes that was produced and broadcast by the CBC that autumn. In the years that followed, I converted the screenplay into this novella.

Steve said he was psychic, and I believed him. Many of the events in *Crystal Balls* are based on things that supposedly actually happened. Some of them I witnessed personally. Most people I talk to about it don't believe Steve was psychic, and indeed they don't believe *anyone* is psychic. Maybe they're right. I don't know. I'm not psychic. Whatever the case may be, *Crystal Balls* was intended to be fun and entertaining, and I hope you enjoyed it.

Bill Rogers
Toronto, January 2013